UNORTHODOX PRACTICES

ααααααααααααααααα

UNORTHODOX PRACTICES

Marissa Piesman

ۋۋۋۋۋۋۋۋۋۋۋۋۋۋۋۋۋ

ACKNOWLEDGMENTS

I would like to thank Barry Lichtenberg, Renee Shanker, and Steven Rabinowitz for their ideas and information. I am also indebted to my literary agent, Janet Manus; my editor, Jane Chelius; my husband, Jeffrey Marks; and my mother, Blanche Piesman; all of whom helped make this book possible.

UNORTHODOX PRACTICES

Chapter One

'M REALLY IN A GROWTH INDUSTRY, thought Nina Fischman, as she divided her phone messages into four separate piles. Now, if only I could force myself to call any of these people back. She tucked a pile under each corner of her phone and spun her chair around to face her wall calendar. It was April and "Wildflowers at the Waterfall" was the Sierra Club centerfold of the month.

Poverty truly was a growth industry in New York these days, and Nina's office was a reflection of the boom. Two walls of her office were lined with file cabinets, on which sat piles of files, obscuring her framed law school diploma and bar admission certificate. The phone rang constantly, mercifully bouncing to the receptionist after three rings. Nina had no time for the phone right now, for today was intake day.

Intake day meant new clients for Nina. Just what she needed. Nina's roster of clients at New York Legal Services Project for Seniors was already choking her. She had what seemed an endless procession of old ladies, shuffling up to her with their walkers and canes, pleading for help. Most of the time, her clients didn't really need a lawyer. They'd do much better with a preacher who could lay his hands upon them, shriek

"Hallelujah," and have them throw away their walkers. Although she had never actually tried laying her hands upon any of her clients, she had a feeling it was not where her talents lay. So she limited herself to phone calls to the Social Security office, applications for food stamps, and appearances in housing court.

Housing court was as close to an evangelical tent as New York City got. The judge sat in front, delivering his sermon, while landlords, tenants, and lawyers packed the pews, speaking in tongues. During Nina's seven-year stint as a housing court attorney, she had seen much moaning, wailing, witnessing, foaming at the mouth, and collapsing to the floor.

As real-estate values in Manhattan soared through the late seventies and the eighties, landlord-tenant relations had become a war zone. Housing court was the major battlefield. Many of Nina's old-lady clients had been living in their apartments since the war. During the fifties and sixties, when middle-class money fled to the suburbs, the landlords treated the older tenants well. Then all of a sudden the space they occupied turned to gold. Anxious to sell the apartments or bump the controlled rent up to market, many landlords got brutal. The bad ones harassed, the better ones bought the tenants out.

Nina's office serviced anyone over sixty-two years of age who lived in New York City. Although there were technically no income restrictions on client eligibility, most of Nina's old ladies were poor. The ones with money often had a lawyer in the family to help them out or were too grand to sit on folding chairs for hours on intake day. The only ones with money were the nut jobs who kept it stuffed in their mattresses and would never pay even a quarter to a shyster lawyer. Because of the office's Manhattan location, it was rare for someone from the outer boroughs to wander in. It did happen, though, and Nina sometimes found herself in Bronx Housing Court, an evangelical tent of smaller though no less intense proportions.

Nina got paid $34,000 a year to protect the elderly from the brutal forces of the marketplace. In addition to her salary, she got a gray metal desk, an orange vinyl swivel chair patched with masking tape, six five-drawer file cabinets (three gray, three green), two phone lines, eight colleagues, and 253 clients. Probably fewer if she would close some of those cases rotting in her file cabinets. But what was the point? She'd close them out and they'd be back a few months later with some other problem. Being poor and old in this town was more than enough to warrant a permanently open case file.

Well, there was one good thing about intake day. It meant no housing court. Nina went down the hall to the basket outside of the paralegal's office and picked up the top file. At that moment the receptionist called to her. "Nina, your mother's on the phone."

"Thanks, I'll take it." Nina's mother was still her specified next of kin and the only one the receptionist would bother to scream down the hall for. Even Grant, Nina's boyfriend of many years, didn't rate the same treatment. Somehow Nina had never bothered to change this state of affairs.

Nina carried the file back with her and opened it as she reached for the phone. "Hi, Ma, what's up?" She read as she talked.

"Are you busy?" asked Ida. Nina never knew how to answer that question. She continually had an endless number of things to do, all mildly urgent. But she never felt busy in the sense of negotiating a tricky deal or meeting with an important client. The way mothers want their children to be busy.

"The usual. I'm about to interview a lady named Bertha Eichner. She lives in Chelsea. Ever hear of her?" Ida, with her seventy years of New York residency, had run across quite a few of Nina's clients. She got around.

"Sorry, dear. Not this time. Well, I won't keep you. I'm

sure Bertha Eichner needs you more than me. I wanted you to come over. I have some new things to show you."

"Let me guess. Did they come from the incinerator room or a neighbor?" Ida cruised her building's garbage daily.

"An ex-neighbor, now deceased."

"Mrs. Gross?" Ida had been to the woman's funeral a few days ago. "Ma, you didn't break into her apartment, did you?"

"Don't be silly. Her daughter was over here, giving everything away. She said none of it would go with her peach and gray living room."

"So what did you get? Furniture or tchotchkes?"

"Oh, a little of everything." Nina could imagine. You could foist anything onto Ida. She had seen her mother happily retrieve used shopping bags, half-dead plants, even old shoes. "Why don't you come over tonight and see for yourself?"

"It's Tuesday, Ma. Group therapy."

"Right. Well, I'm busy the rest of the week. Try to stop by on the weekend." Ida was often booked.

"I'll see you on Saturday morning, how's that?"

"Very good. And take good care of Bertha."

Bertha Eichner turned out to be easy. She was one of those rare specimens who had no housing problems. She lived in one of those union projects built at a time when the word co-op still had progressive, not entrepreneurial overtones. That's what Nina wanted more of, tenants without landlords. All Bertha needed was some help with a Medicaid problem and a few minutes of chat. Nina had learned early on to set limits for the chat. "We have only a few minutes left. Is there anything else you'd like to discuss?" If the shrinks could do it, she could, too. It usually worked. The client obediently wound down and it was on to the next. And there was always an endless procession of nexts.

2

NINA SURVEYED THE CONTENTS of her mother's refrigerator. It was a habit left over from childhood, standing there with the refrigerator door open. Like watching television. Watching refrigerator, Nina called it. She only did it in her mother's house. Judging from the contents, Ida was in one of her Weight Watcher phases. Mini pita breads, Light 'n Lively cottage cheese, a bowl of apples, and a tub of diet margarine. Nothing interesting. She opened a Tupperware container hopefully. Homemade gefilte fish. That's weird, Nina thought. She'd never known her mother to make gefilte fish. It was too much trouble, going to the fish store to get ground carp and all. She grabbed an apple and closed the refrigerator. "Ma," she called to Ida, who was in the other room, "what's with the gefilte fish?"

Ida came into the kitchen. "Mrs. Gross's daughter gave it to me after the funeral. I guess her mother had made it for Passover." The Fischmans hadn't really celebrated Passover since Ida's mother died, but it remained one of Nina's favorite holidays. She much preferred the ones with the seven-course dinners to the ones with the compulsory fasting. This year the leftover gefilte fish was the first physical evidence of Passover that Nina had seen.

"Didn't you feel a little strange taking a dead woman's gefilte fish?"

"Never mind the gefilte fish. Look at this." Ida opened the door to a kitchen cabinet.

"Look at what?" To Nina the shelves looked much as they had for the past three decades, stuffed to the gills with jars, cans, and boxes of every conceivable description. The groceries were in double layers, the way overloaded bookshelves looked. Everything open was wrapped in plastic bags to protect against the roaches. Nina recognized the same useless items that Ida had bought decades ago in the Bronx and had moved to Manhattan with her, anticipating an eventual found use. Things like cans of french-fried onion rings for the tuna-noodle casserole that Ida just couldn't bring herself to make.

"Look at my new kosher foods section." Ida proudly pointed to an array of Streit's and Horowitz Margareten products crammed in among her more traditional collection.

Nina shook her head. "You're shameless. What are you going to do with a half-empty box of matzoh meal? When's the last time you whipped up a potato kugel, anyway?" Ida had left her religion behind at Hunter College back in the thirties. With it she had likewise disposed of ethnic cuisine.

"You never know. Lots of people return to their roots the closer they get to death."

Nina appraised her mother for signs of her impending demise. Even though Ida had recently passed seventy, she looked pretty far from death. Because she had never been a glamorous type, she hadn't seemed to age much at all. She looked the same as she always had, sensible and sturdy. The retired schoolteacher look wasn't really different from the schoolteacher look. Ida led Nina into the living room. "Look at this." She pointed to a small Queen Anne chair covered in hideous avocado brocade.

"Is that also from the Mrs. Gross collection?"

"Yup. I think it has potential. We'll see what Laura can do with it." Nina's younger sister was a doctor's wife, a mother of two, and a part-time furniture restorer. Nina called her the Queen of the Strippers.

"Laura's good, isn't she?"

Ida nodded. "She's very patient."

"Some people think that's a virtue." Nina found it tiresome to have one of those quiet, thin, modest, neat types for a sister. Ida, on the other hand, took pride in her younger daughter but couldn't imagine where in the world she had come from.

"The person who really just got a windfall is Rabinowitz," continued Nina. "He's been waiting to sell that apartment for years. Jesus, I wonder what it's worth now? Three bedrooms, two and half baths, faces west. Definitely over half a million. What do you think? You're the maven. Six? Six and a half?"

Ida sat down to think. Her favorite subject had just come up and she was savoring it. That was the great thing about being obsessed with real estate in New York these days. You didn't have to manipulate the conversation to bring up the topic. You could count on it to just naturally arise about every ten minutes.

Ida Fischman hadn't been born a real-estate maven. She was a late bloomer. No one knew from it in her youth on the Lower East Side and even after the war, when people were marching off to the suburbs, having their first encounters with home ownership. Ida and her husband, Leo, had stayed put in the Bronx. They just couldn't see themselves out on Exit 45 of the Long Island Expressway, wearing Bermuda shorts and mowing the lawn. Ida and Leo were like cockroaches, indigenous to the New York apartment. So they stayed put. And the Bronx, that beautiful borough of Art Deco apartment houses and stately parks and grand boulevards, slowly burned down. The children Ida taught stopped listening, and Alexander's department store began selling schlock. Leo barely noticed. It had been downhill for him, anyway, ever since the days of radical politics in the City College cafeteria. The Communist party had broken his heart so badly he never expected much from anything again. It became increasingly difficult to get him to put down the paper, much less leave the Bronx.

Ida, on the other hand, had plans. "We must move to Manhattan" became her litany. No one took her seriously. She reminded Nina of Chekhov's three sisters with their "We must go to Moscow" obsession. But one day, while Nina was still in law school and Laura was just finished with college, Ida had an announcement. A client of Ida's brother (the lawyer brother, not the accountant brother) had a vacancy, and Ida had signed a three-year lease. The Fischmans were moving out of the Diaspora and into the Holy Land. The Upper West Side.

The Upper West Side in the mid-seventies might not have seemed like the Promised Land to everybody else, but it certainly did to Ida. She was leaving a street where women spent the afternoon staring out of their windows, clad in housedresses that buttoned down the front, locally referred to as "dusters." Ida never wanted to see a woman dressed in a duster again. She wanted to promenade down West End Avenue with elderly German Jews dressed in loden coats. She wanted to sit on the fountain in Lincoln Center and watch elegantly dressed couples hop into cabs headed east. She wanted to mingle with gay men in the antique stores on Columbus Avenue and with graduate students in the Chinese restaurants on Broadway.

The building the Fischmans moved into was a solid pre-war in the middle of dozens of other solid pre-wars that constituted the canyon that was West End Avenue. The lobby was shabby, the picture molding was lumpy, and the cockroach infestation was worse than in the Bronx. But Ida loved it. To her, every chip of peeling paint, every worn spot in the lobby marble, represented the intelligentsia. She was in heaven.

A year later Leo was dead. Public opinion had it that it was the move from the Bronx that killed him. That he was a sort of reverse hothouse flower, a straggly street weed that couldn't survive in an elevator building. But Ida felt a sense of inevitability about it: Jewish men of Leo's generation weren't built for the long haul. She'd been watching her friends' husbands die for years now. She hoped that the next generation would last longer. Maybe all that squash playing they did would pay off. Besides, the sons had clients instead of customers and didn't have to spend their lives locked up in the shop screaming at their partners. Although the ones on the subway with their squash racquets usually looked as miserable as Leo did while he was going through bankruptcy proceedings.

Ida made a good widow. She retired and had a large network of friends, mostly other widowed retired schoolteachers. They were all geniuses at absorbing New York culture at half-price. They had seen every ballet and museum exhibit. These ladies with their support hose and Channel 13 tote bags lived lives straight out of New York magazine.

In the midst of this whirlwind widowhood, Ida's building was converted from a rental to a co-op. Co-ops were showing up everywhere in Manhattan. Across the country, condominiums were becoming an established form of home ownership. New York had to do it differently, of course, creating corporations and shareholders and giving everyone the right to interfere when their neighbors wanted to sell their apartments. New Yorkers liked to make a profit, but they wouldn't sell their right to interfere for any price.

The family wanted Ida to buy. Laura's husband was hot on

Upper West Side property as an investment. "Thirty grand might seem like a lot to you now," Ken said, "but you'll be able to sell it for ten times that amount when the market peaks in a few years. I promise."

Nina was equally encouraging about the purchase. "Don't be an asshole," she had said. "Learn a lesson from my clients. If you don't buy, there are only two things that can happen to you. Either the landlord will stop doing repairs and start treating you like shit or a neighbor will buy your apartment, hoping to expand when you finally die. Do you want to have your next-door neighbor sniffing for signs of your impending demise every time you step into the hallway to go to the incinerator room?" They were actually compactor rooms by this time, but Nina, like most native New Yorkers, refused to update her terminology. The way that a lot of people in town still considered the Mets an expansion team. "For once in your life do something smart," Nina harangued. "You're in an appreciating market. Buy."

So Ida bought. And the $30,000 apartment became a $300,000 apartment.

Ida watched the new owners in her building arrive in waves. First came the lawyer-shrink couples, then the lawyer-lawyer couples. As prices started to nudge the half-million mark, a whole new crowd showed up. Bankers. WASPs. All kinds of people. And Zabar's wasn't a herring store anymore.

Ida rolled with the punches. She considered these recent arrivals a little tall, blond, and bland for her taste, a new breed of New York *übermenschen*. But she appreciated the fact that they made good co-op shareholders. They were smart, organized, and reasonable. A pleasure doing business with. So what if they weren't colorful? Who wanted to be in business with someone colorful? Leo had a colorful partner once. The IRS got him. And so what if Zabar's had become the Library of Congress for balsamic vinegar? Ida did not live by herring alone.

In New York the favorite question these days was undoubtedly "What's it worth?" Asked with lip-smacking satis-faction by those who owned and helpless alarm by those who rented. Nina was somewhere in between. Although she still rented, she enjoyed watching her mother's asset appreciate. So her question about the value of Mrs. Gross's apartment carried elements of both glee and despair.

Ida had a ready answer. "The last apartment in the build-ing with a similar share allocation went for six seventy-five. But that was a totally renovated resale, with a Poggenpohl kitchen and marble in the bathroom."

Mrs. Gross had never bought her apartment, but had stayed on as a tenant. Even in eviction plans, such as this was, non-purchasing senior citizens could remain as renters for life. The landlord—or sponsor, as he was referred to in the context of a conversion—could hold on to the apartment or sell it, whichever he chose. The only thing he couldn't do was evict the elderly tenant. Eviction plans became rare once the legal requirements were stiffened, and non-eviction became the more common form. But on West End Avenue in the 1970s they had still been the rule. "Mrs. Gross's apartment will go for a lot less. It's a total wreck."

"Well, I wouldn't exactly expect Rabinowitz to give her a Poggenpohl kitchen." Nina wasn't exactly sure what Poggenpohl was, but it had a state-of-the-art sound. Some-times Nina missed the old Bronx Ida, who didn't casually toss around names like Poggenpohl.

"Rabinowitz doesn't own that apartment anymore," Ida said. "After the building was converted, he sold Mrs. Gross's apartment to a Netherlands Antilles corporation. It must be three or four years ago by now."

Nina was surprised that a foreign corporation would invest in an occupied building on the Upper West Side. They usually did bigger deals like new-construction East Side high-rises. "Who are the principals?" she asked.

"God knows. You know how these shells are. Shells within shells." Ida used the word *shells* much the way she used the name *Poggenpohl*. "All I know is that we get the maintenance check from some attorney named Myron Kaplan who has an office in the Lincoln Building on Forty-second Street." Ida had been on the co-op board of directors for several years now and had access to all kinds of information.

"Is he a principal?"

"I doubt it. They're usually foreigners, aren't they?"

"I think so." Nina wasn't exactly an expert on corporate law. There was very little call for it in her line of work. "Maybe Ferdinand and Imelda own it. Anyway, you'll know the price soon enough. You are going to stay on the board, aren't you?"

"Absolutely. Someone's got to give these people some perspective about these things. It's amazing how narrow-minded the latest crop are. Like they went straight from third grade to business school. What was that term you kids used to use? 'Mind expansion.' What ever happened to mind expansion?"

Nina smiled. "My generation is desperately trying to contract their minds enough to make a living."

"Well, I did always feel that some of your minds had expanded a bit much. Into entropy. But these people's minds have contracted into hard little walnuts. I'll give them one thing, though. They are good at making a living. No problems there."

"You have a lot more respect for them than you used to," Nina reminded her mother. "Don't forget that you were the person who ridiculed them for buying retail."

"Well, at the time I thought they had overpaid. Who knew that their apartments would double all over again?"

"They must have known. And your son-in-law, the awesome real-estate genius and dermatologist, told you so."

"I'll admit I called that one wrong. But I got smarter.

Look, Nina, it's taken me decades of psychotherapy to understand the meaning of 'Nothing ventured, nothing gained.' It wasn't the way Daddy and I lived our lives. Don't fall into the same trap."

Nina steered her mother away from sentiment. She wasn't in the mood. "One trap I'm not going to fall into is twenty-three years of psychotherapy." Ida was well into her third decade of treatment. "If I'm still going by then, I'll terminate and convert to Catholicism."

"You'd make a lousy Catholic. You're much more suited to worshiping at the altar of psychotherapy."

She sighed. Her mother was right. But it was getting trite already. She tried to imagine terminating. It was a stretch, like imagining herself married or a mother or thin. Directions she had supposedly been moving in for a lifetime, with no real expectations of ever getting there.

"Time for tea," said Ida. It was a genteel way of saying there was no reason to wait for mealtime to eat. "Let's have some of Mrs. Gross's macaroons."

"I'm shocked. Judging by your refrigerator, I'd say you're on your first week of Weight Watchers."

"It's true, it's true. But sometimes I can't stand it anymore. Fifty-five years of dieting. First Sucaryl, then Sweet'n Low, now Equal. Barrels of cottage cheese. Citrus groves of grapefruits. For what? I'm still a short dumpy lady. Except now, after all these years, I'm a short dumpy old lady. What would be so terrible if I just gave it up? You think it would really make a difference?"

"Don't be ridiculous. For women like us, dieting isn't something you suddenly decide not to do. It's something we just do. Even if it doesn't work. Especially since it doesn't work. If it worked, we wouldn't have to do it anymore."

"But it's pointless."

"Look, it's like breathing. You can hold your breath for a

few moments the way you can eat a couple of macaroons once in a while. But there's no such thing as stopping doing it. You can't suddenly grant yourself an exemption. It's who we are. We're dieters." Privately Nina wondered if she was talking about dieting or psychotherapy. Probably both. Too bad. Dieting was cheaper, unless you got into the spa circuit. Then the bills could top even five-mornings-a-week analysis on Park Avenue.

Ida was shaking her head and moaning. "Endless," she groaned.

Nina tried to say something encouraging. "Ma, as far as being dumpy goes, believe me, I've seen a lot dumpier." Both Nina and Ida were noticeably pear-shaped, with less than fabulous legs. But neither could be characterized as fat, except possibly in southern California. "Besides, you're not bad for a Jewish girl. Name one Jewish woman who has no food issues."

"Laura," Ida responded promptly.

"True. Naturally thin, but enjoys food. Wonderful cook. Keeps a full larder but never invades it inappropriately. It's sickening. Sometimes I wonder if it's harder to have her as a sister or a daughter."

"Or a mother."

Nina thought about her niece. It was too soon to tell if Danielle was going to be a chub. She wasn't fat, but she certainly showed signs of inheriting the loudmouth gene that had passed Laura by. "Maybe the kid will grow up thin and lovely and she'll spend a painless adolescence shopping with her mother."

"She's got a shot at it."

"Anyway, why not break out the macaroons? After all, I wouldn't want my weight to slip below my IQ."

"God forbid," said Ida, as she went to fetch a can opener for the macaroon tin.

3

NINA STARED AT THE HEADINGS on the Chinese menu. Pork. Chicken. Beef. Seafood. Noodles. Each gave her a little thrill. Nina felt a certain way in Chinese restaurants. A way she felt nowhere else. The way an old-time alkie must feel in a broken-down gin mill. A sense of familiarity and comfort tinged with guilt. Only around Chinese food did Nina drop even a semblance of vigilance and eat like a pig. Like Aunt Sophie at the Viennese table at a bar mitzvah. Like Albert Finney in *Tom Jones*. Like the girls in the dorm on a heavy marijuana night. There had been a lot of magazine talk lately about comfort food. Cookbooks written on mashed potatoes, chicken pot pie, and macaroni and cheese. Shrimp with lobster sauce was Nina's comfort food. It certainly tasted better than anything her mother had ever actually cooked.

Grant, on the other hand, never bothered to look at the menu. He let Nina order. He didn't see Chinese food as anything transcendental. It was just food, for chrissakes. A little greasy for his taste, actually. But he was tolerant about food craziness. He had to be. He had been dating Jewish women exclusively since his freshman year at Madison.

Before that he had gone out with no one. Tall, thin, painfully shy, and the son of a Lutheran minister, Grant Miller wasn't exactly a heartthrob in his Milwaukee high school. But when he got to the University of Wisconsin, he found hordes of New York Jewish girls lusting after his pale scarecrow body. He remained hooked. Why ruin a good thing? He found them smart, funny, and sexy. There was a lushness about them, compared to the girls he had grown up with. Generously endowed with everything—words, ideas, noses, and breasts. He liked the fact that they usually had some extra weight on them. He even got a kick out of watching their bodies shrink and plump up again as they switched from grapefruit back to Szechuan shrimp.

Nina and Grant had been a couple in their own way for almost five years now. They had never lived together. She couldn't be persuaded to give up the Upper West Side, and he couldn't bear to leave the Lower East. They both wondered what would happen next, Nina in her obsessive, agonizing way, Grant in his laconic way. But neither took any action to move the plot along.

Grant was a poverty lawyer also. They had met when they were both working at the Legal Services Project for Seniors. Grant had left to start up the Haitian Refugee Relief Project in Brooklyn. Nina sometimes thought about how many people she knew who worked for projects. Twenty years ago the word had had a nice ring to it, like the Blues Project. Now it sounded dismal, like a housing project.

Nina turned her attention from the menu to Grant and their friends Terry and Steve. Steve was a colleague of Nina's and also Grant's best friend. Terry, his wife, was the only one at the table who did not work for a project. She worked for a gossip weekly. When she had married Steve she was still a secretary. Not another shikse-secretary-nabs-Jewish-lawyer scenario, they all said. And Terry and Steve looked the part, he with his dark beard, horn-rimmed glasses, and brooding air. She with her post-cheerleader cheerfulness and contact lenses. But now Terry earned three times as much as anyone else at the table. She had clawed her way out from behind the typewriter at the gossip weekly and climbed up to a substantial editorial position with glamorous lunches and international travel.

Nina adored Terry. She found everything she said fascinating. She could listen endlessly to who used to be married to whom, who was gay, and how many cosmetic surgical procedures Cher had had. Thank God for Terry, since Grant and Steve could talk about housing court all night. You'd think it was the White House. This evening was no exception. After they ordered, the conversation zoomed right back.

Grant and Steve were discussing Judge Spielberg, who was being temporarily assigned to a hearing part in housing court. "Have you ever appeared in front of him?" Grant asked Steve.

"Sure. He's not a bad guy. He can actually be pretty pro-tenant, but he doesn't like to feel that you're manipulating him. If he does, he can turn on you. Nina, you've appeared before him, haven't you?"

Nina and Terry were deeply absorbed in discussing the sexuality of a famous talk-show host. Terry had just told Nina that his sexual preference ran toward cue-card boys. As a result, Nina hadn't heard Steve's question. "Who? What?" she asked.

"What do you think of Spielberg?" he asked.

"A brat with a camera. Did I ever tell you the story about watching him film *Jaws* on the Vineyard? It was Memorial Day weekend, in '74, 1 think. I was sitting next to his father..." Nina enjoyed pretending that she was at the Polo Lounge, gossiping about the industry.

Grant groaned. "We've heard this story several times.

There's no need to tell it again. Nina, listen to me carefully. We are not discussing Steven Spielberg, we're talking about Judge Spielberg. Harry Spielberg. What do you think of him?"

"Oh, him." Her animation ebbed. "He's okay. He's got a great mustache."

"Real substantive type, isn't she?" Steve said to Grant.

Grant dismissed her with a wave. "Trying to get Nina to keep her mind on the law is like trying to get her to give up Chinese food. There's no point."

Terry put her hand on Nina's arm. "Why did you go to law school? I've never quite understood."

Nina had been asked that question so many times that she had once sat down and compiled a list of reasons. It read as follows:

1. I decided that if I had to be a secretary one more day I was going to crack the typewriter over my boss's head.
2. I wanted to earn my age in thousands per year.
3. What else is an English major supposed to do? Open an English store?
4. Law school is what good girls did in the seventies. Like being virgins on their wedding day in the fifties.
5. It was an escape. Sort of the marijuana of the post-Vietnam generation.
6. I got a good score on the LSATs, and I didn't want to waste it.

She decided to spare them. So she just shrugged and said to Terry, "Well, you've gotta make a living."

"She really does hate housing court," Grant said. "On days when she has an appearance scheduled, she gets up and says 'Should I go to court today or kill myself?'"

"But housing court is so much fun," Steve said. "It's such a game."

"Yeah, a game of male mutual masturbation," Nina snapped back, just as the waiter arrived with the food. It put her in a better mood.

"Speaking of jerking off in housing court," Steve said, "I have some sad news. One of my favorite clients, Mrs. Kahn, died last week."

Nina had a dim recollection of a short old lady who wore hats. Grant remembered her, too. "You mean that non-purchasing tenant on West End Avenue who kept conducting her own personal rent strikes?" he asked.

"That's right. I never thought she could go. Such a tough old lady. Apparently it was a surprise to everyone. Her daughter called me to cancel a court appearance we had scheduled. She told me that Mrs. Kahn's doctor had thought she wouldn't give out until she hit a hundred."

"Well, I guess Mrs. Kahn has conducted her last rent strike, huh?" Grant said.

"I guess so. But the last one was wild. The building converted to a co-op a couple of years ago, and of course Mrs. Kahn never bought. I guess the landlord wanted to unload her apartment, because he sold it to some investors, who technically became her landlord. Well, Kahn didn't care who she withheld rent from, right? A warranty of habitability is a warranty of habitability, right? And her apartment was pretty bad. The kitchen, the bathroom, all the walls—everything was a mess. The only problem she didn't have was cockroaches. So she withholds her rent and gets a dispossess notice. This time the petitioner is the investor group that bought the apartment, West Estates, N.V. And they send this third-year associate from Case and Clark down to housing court. There he is, H. Pennington Wells or something, in his navy blue suit, wearing that look of smug distaste that they all have when they have to do an eviction. The look that says 'I don't generally appear in courts of limited jurisdiction.'"

"I love blowing those guys away," Grant said. "After five minutes in housing court, they're usually on the verge of tears."

"This guy was a classic. I walk over to him while we're still in the hall—"

Nina's eyes suddenly unglazed and she interrupted. "What was the petitioner's name again?"

Grant rolled his eyes. "What difference does that make?"

Terry defended her. "When Nina gets that cub-reporter look, there's usually a point to her questions. She has finely honed journalistic instincts."

"West Estates, N.V.," said Steve. "Why do you want to know?"

"N.V. That means it's a Netherlands Antilles corporation, doesn't it?"

Steve nodded.

Nina shook her head. "I don't get it. What's with all these Netherlands Antilles corporations suddenly buying occupied apartments? My mother just told me that her neighbor's apartment was bought by one also. I always thought that N.V. corporations were shells for big foreign money. Where a desire for tax benefits, anonymity, and easy dissolution made it worthwhile to go to all the trouble of incorporating down in Curaçao. Not for two-bit deals like buying an occupied apartment on West End Avenue."

"I'm sure they didn't incorporate solely for the purpose of buying Mrs. Kahn's apartment," Steve said. "They probably already own a lot of real estate in New York and picked this up along the way. This just means that a different kind of investor is getting into the occupied-apartment market. Foreigners."

"Goys," said Grant. He liked to show off his Yiddish.

"The plural is *goyim*." Nina liked to correct Grant's

Yiddish. "Anyway, how do you find out who the principals are in these deals? Just out of curiosity."

"It's almost impossible," Steve answered. "In order for a Netherlands Antilles corporation to own real estate in New York, they have to qualify to do business here. Which means that under section thirteen-oh-four of the Business Corporation Law they have to do the usual designation of the secretary of state for service of process." Nina's eyes started to glaze over, but Steve went on. "Their attorney can sign the application for doing business. And a managing agent from a Curaçao bank is usually named as the corporation's registered agent. There's no requirement under thirteen-oh-four that an officer of the corporation sign anything."

Nina couldn't believe it. "What are you, some kind of idiot savant? You're a poverty lawyer, for God's sake. What the hell are you supposed to know about foreign corporations and the BCL?"

"I think it's kind of fascinating," Steve replied.

"I wish I thought it was kind of fascinating," Nina wailed. "I have the mind of a gossip columnist trapped within the body of a lawyer. Now I know how transsexuals feel."

"Stop it," said Grant. "You're a good lawyer. If you had to know about the Business Corporation Law, you'd know about it."

"Maybe you're just not interested in what you're doing," said Terry. "Maybe you need to—"

Nina cut her off. "Here it comes, the 'law in all its infinite possibilities' speech."

"Well, it is a pretty broad field," Terry said. "I'm sure you could find an area that interests you."

"You know I've heard that exact line from dozens of people. And, funny thing, not one of them was a lawyer. They were all either shrinks or married to doctors. Lawyers know better." She morosely wrapped a moo shu pancake. But she couldn't pout for too long. The briefest lag in conversation made her extremely nervous. Even if she was being morose, it had to be in an upbeat way. "If I could do anything, and if money was no issue, you know what my dream job would be? Subway counseling. I'd have a little booth and people would come up to me and ask me what was the quickest way from one stop to another stop. I love figuring out ways to get places on the subway."

"That would be interesting for about twenty minutes. Then you'd get sick of it," Terry said.

"You're probably right," she agreed. "What's your dream job?"

Terry looked embarrassed. "The one I have."

Nina tried to imagine feeling that way. To feel utterly content. About anything. It was unimaginable.

4

WHEN DID HER SISTER START lighting Shabbos candles? She stared at Laura's covered head. It was so incongruous. Nina couldn't remember even being in a room with someone lighting Shabbos candles. Except maybe her grandmother thirty years ago. And now here was her own sister doing it. Nina and Laura had been brought up with a fierce distaste for religion, the opiate of the masses and all that. And as far as cultural Judaism went, Laura had always been more out of it than her older sister. Nina had picked up a lot from her grandparents, from books, from the general Bronx atmosphere. Laura had seemed impervious.

Nina looked around at her sister's dining room. It was a very beautiful room. The original picture moldings and baseboards were mahogany and had been carefully stripped and refinished by Laura. The brownstone dated from the 1870s and was wider than your typical Brooklyn row house. Therefore, the room could accommodate the ponderous Victorian dining room set Laura had picked up at an auction. She had stripped and refinished the table and chairs herself, although she'd finally relented and had the intricately carved sideboard dipped. She had also upholstered the chairs and whipped up matching balloon shades for the windows. Laura was always whipping things up. Balloon shades, soufflés, mother-daughter outfits. Nina spent an equal amount of time whipping herself up into a frenzy. Actually, the covered head and Shabbos candles looked appropriate in the Victorian room. Nina privately wondered if Laura considered this ritual simply a design accessory.

"Since when did you start lighting Shabbos candles?"

"Oh, I've been doing this for a few months." Laura opened a drawer of the sideboard and pulled out a box of matches.

"How come?"

"Danielle had a sleep-over at her friend's, and Rachel's mom lit them. She was very impressed and couldn't stop talking about it. I thought it would be nice for the family if we did, too."

"Next you'll be joining the Garfield Temple."

"We already have."

"You're kidding."

"It's mostly for the pool."

Nina continued to stare at her sister incredulously. "These things happen," Laura assured her.

"Not in my family."

"The truth is that I missed all this stuff when we were growing up. You did, too, but you won't admit it."

"I don't know about that."

"Kids just want to be like everyone else. So why should I put mine through all that atheist torture we had to go through? Let them have an easier time."

"Daddy's rolling in his grave. Besides, even if I wanted to become a practicing Jew, I wouldn't know where to start. How many candles do you light and what prayer do you say? Where did you get the candlesticks? How do you know all this?"

"At least you know some Yiddish," Laura said. "I don't know any."

"Why is that, I've always wondered? We grew up in the same house, didn't we?"

"I don't know, but when I signed up for Beginning Jewish Ed, I knew so little that the teacher assumed I had recently converted. It was mortifying."

Nina scrutinized her sister. Despite a bit of generosity of nose, she could pass. Nina, though blonder and smaller of nose, could never pass. Once a friend's husband claimed not to know Nina was Jewish. The friend laughed when she told Nina the story and said, "Don't worry, he didn't realize Jackie Mason was Jewish, either."

"Would you do me a favor?" said Laura. "Go upstairs and tell everybody to come down."

"Sure." As she climbed the two flights of stairs to the family room, Nina paused on the parlor floor. It contained two well-proportioned rooms connected by French doors. Here, too, the moldings and baseboards had been stripped, as had the mahogany spindles and the banister. The rooms contained a baby grand piano and several overstuffed pieces covered in chintz. At the rear, a window seat overlooked the garden, which featured daffodils at the moment. The brass sconces that lit the room were original gas fixtures. It could have just as easily been the home of a Victorian family as that of a Jewish dermatologist in the late twentieth century. As a child, Nina had read books like *Alice in Wonderland* over and over and had longed to be a Victorian child in a pinafore making daisy chains. As an adult she realized that if she had been born a hundred years earlier she would have been plucking chickens in the shtetl with a schmatta on her head. But the pinafore feeling always hit her on her sister's parlor floor.

Up one flight were the family room and the master bedroom. Nina peeked into the bedroom on her way to fetch the family. The same brass sconces were there, and the room was a swirl of Victorian hearts and lace. The bedclothes reminded

Nina of the Victorian pinafores she used to fantasize about. In fact, the bedclothes seemed to change each time she came over. That bed had a better wardrobe than she did.

In the family room, Ken and Ida and the two kids were watching a videotape of *Lady and the Tramp*. Danielle was almost four. Jared was a year and a half. Nina had never forgiven her sister for giving the kids such lousy names. Trendy in the worst way. The kind of names that go in and out of fashion in less than a year. Walking around with names like that was like having the year of your birth tattooed on your forehead, the way a harvest gold kitchen screamed 1959. As far as Nina was concerned, Danielle was only one step above Tiffany. Unless you actually lived in France, where it was probably more akin to Elizabeth.

Nina announced dinner, but they all seemed reluctant to turn off the VCR. She watched a few minutes with them. It was pretty good stuff. Ida tried to turn it off, but Danielle had to show her the right button. As they all went down the stairs, Ken asked where Grant was. He wasn't particularly fond of Grant, but he sometimes found his presence comforting. Usually the only other male in the room was seventeen months old.

"Running around with the Haitians, I think. He said something about a fund-raiser."

Actually Nina hated bringing Grant to her sister's house. He looked all wrong there, the way a chrome and glass coffee table would have looked on the parlor floor.

Laura did a cute little number with the Shabbos candles, covering Danielle's head and having her participate. Then Laura wheeled out an antique serving cart filled with antique platters of food. There was a roast surrounded by clumps of perfect baby vegetables. If Ken dropped dead, her sister could always get a job as a food stylist. Nina pondered the roast. She herself had never purchased a roast. She once tried but was overcome by anxiety. Everyone told her the first thing to do was go to a butcher you could trust. She really wasn't that intimate with any butchers, and in the supermarket, the large hunks of meat had labels on them that conveyed no meaningful information to her. She didn't know whether she wanted bone in or out. There were just too many options. It was like buying a car. They should have roast magazines for people like her to read so they could make informed decisions. Instead of *Road and Track*, she could subscribe to *Oven and Rack*. Because she had to face facts. In this decade you just couldn't get away with serving vegetarian lasagna anymore.

"Where's Grant?" asked Laura. She wasn't particularly fond of him, either, but she bent over backward to be open-minded and take him seriously. The bending over backward had started only after numerous "you just want me to marry a doctor" screaming sessions.

"Working." Nina dug an antique silver serving spoon into a mound of orange mush.

"What's this?"

"Carrot and peanut puree. Are you two getting married?" Laura asked.

"I don't know. I don't think so." Nina couldn't picture herself marrying anyone. She had been checking the single box on insurance forms for so long that she couldn't imagine doing anything else.

"It's been years." Laura pressed on. "How long has it been?"

"About five."

"And you're going to be thirty-five in June, unless I have my dates wrong." Laura surveyed her sister's head for gray hair. There was quite a bit, but the gray didn't show up distinctly in Nina's ashy hair. It was more like a suggestion of gray.

"Well, I've never lived my life the way you have."

"What do you mean by the way I have?"

"Next I'm going to do this. One-two-three-go."

Laura gave a small but derisive laugh. "That's an understatement."

"I know a G.I. man you might be interested in going out with," offered Ken.

"You mean the army?" Ida asked with alarm.

"Gastrointestinal."

Danielle suddenly screamed. "Mommy, there's an ear in my meat. It's gross."

Laura inspected the offending object. "Dear, that's a dried apricot. It's not an ear, it's a fruit. Go ahead and try it. It's yummy, like raisins."

"Laura, this purée is delicious," said Ida. "Is it from one of the *Sixty Minute Gourmets*?"

"No, I'm off Franey. This is from the *Silver Palate Good Times Cookbook*. My new bible."

"Those are the people who own that store on Columbus Avenue that throw blueberry chutney onto everything," said Nina.

"I actually have some Silver Palate blueberry chutney," Ida said. "From Mrs. Gross. My neighbor who just died."

"I never exactly thought of her as the Silver Palate type," said Nina.

"I have no idea where it came from, but there among the kosher debris her daughter foisted upon me was an unopened jar of Silver Palate blueberry chutney."

"It's probably a gift that she got and never used," said Laura.

"Yeah, like fruitcake," said Nina. "I once read an article about what people do with the fruitcakes they get at Christmas. It was truly amazing. They had stories about people who had kept them in their freezers for decades. And a lot of people recycle them. Some fruitcakes change hands several times in one Christmas season."

"Mommy, what's a fruitcake?" asked Danielle.

Ken answered. "Your Aunt Nina's a fruitcake," he said.

Nina patted her hair and said in a Mae West voice, "I have been known to change hands several times in one season."

Ida shook her head and gave an *oi vey* mutter. Then she said, "I'm not surprised that Mrs. Gross never opened her blueberry chutney. She was a real health nut and very vain about her weight. She never baked and wouldn't eat prepared foods."

"What about those macaroons we destroyed?"

"They were also unopened. Remember?"

"True." Nina nodded. "Ma, I've been meaning to ask you. What's the name of the Netherlands Antilles corporation that owns Mrs. Gross's apartment?"

"West Estates. Why?"

"That's it. It's the same one. This guy who works in my office—you've met Steve, haven't you?"

"The one with the gorgeous wife?" asked Ida.

"Thin, Ma, not gorgeous."

"Sorry, sometimes the distinction blurs."

"You should go into a consciousness-raising group for fatties. Anyway, Steve had a client, Mrs. Kahn, who dropped dead very suddenly. Her heart gave out, just like Mrs. Gross. And guess what? She was also a non-purchasing tenant in an apartment on West End Avenue owned by West Estates. Do you think it's more than a coincidence?"

Ken shook his head. "Don't be ridiculous. More than a coincidence that two old ladies die of cardiac arrest? It doesn't even rise to the level of a coincidence. That's what old ladies die of, unless they die of cancer."

"Please," snapped Laura. "Am I going to have to put the kids to bed?"

"Don't want them to hear the C-word, huh?" said Nina, mockingly.

Ken ignored both of them. He turned his attention to Ida. "What do you think Gross's apartment will go for?"

It seemed as if she had been asked that question a hundred times in the past week. "Can we go back a step?" Ida said. "I don't think it's more than a coincidence that both Mrs. Kahn and Mrs. Gross dropped dead of a heart attack. But Mrs. Gross did die very unexpectedly. I was talking to Beatrice Frank, one of the more ghoulish yentas in the building. And she went into great detail about how Mrs. Gross's doctor was so surprised because he thought she'd live to be a hundred."

"Those are the exact same words that Steve used about Mrs. Kahn," Nina pointed out.

"Look," said Ken, "it happens. How many times in your life have you heard that phrase—thought she would live to be a hundred?"

"A hundred," said Nina.

"So what is this big coincidence? A foreign corporation goes into the business of buying co-op apartments occupied by old ladies, gambling on their early death. When the old ladies finally die, people say the same thing they always do: 'We all thought she'd live to be a hundred.' The only coincidence here is that Nina had mutual acquaintances of both old ladies."

"Some coincidence," said Laura. "Nina has mutual acquaintances of the entire Upper West Side."

"Now can we discuss something important?" Ken said. "Like whether I should buy Mrs. Gross's apartment?"

Laura got alarmed. "What are you talking about? I am not letting you move this family into Manhattan. I'm not leaving the Slope or this house. Not after all these years spent stripping all this wood. And Danielle loves her nursery school. And I've just gotten Jared into a great play group. Don't even think about it."

"Calm down. We're not moving. I love it here. You know me, I'm a Slope kind of guy."

"So why are you talking about buying an apartment on West End Avenue?"

"I know West Side residential property seems high now, but I think it's going to go even higher. I thought we could sublet the West Side apartment for a while and then resell when the market peaks."

"Sublet?" said Nina. "Mom's co-op board thinks sublet is a dirty word."

"We have occasionally granted permission to sublet. Under the right circumstances," said Ida.

"And will undoubtedly continue to do so," said Ken. "Ida has great influence in that building. I'm sure she can get the board to grant consent. Ida, if you'd prefer, I can put the apartment in the children's names."

"Jesus, Ken," said Nina, "don't be so high-handed. What are you, a healer of souls or a corporate raider?"

"Maybe a little of both," said Ida.

"Since when did you become such a medical capitalist?" Nina continued. "Whatever happened to Dr. Kenneth Scott Rubin, the sweet dermatologist who used to bore us to death talking about people's rashes?"

The truth was that Ken had been spending more time on finances and less time on medicine and he missed it. He loved being a doctor. He had wanted to be one ever since he was little. Not that he had been one of those nerdy science types who wore slide rule tie clips in junior high. Not him. He had been a regular Long Island kid who played a decent game of basketball. He had a crew cut, then a JFK. Later, when he got to college, he let his hair grow longer and smoked some dope to be sociable. But he stayed pre-med and worked hard and did well.

Nina claimed you could tell the bio majors in college by the big watches they wore. Ken was a big watch kind of guy. Nina hadn't known people who wore watches. It was too much responsibility to remember to wind them. This was before they had invented the self-winding kind. Back then, people had a tendency to sleep through eleven o'clock classes. On campus, if someone asked you the time, a popular response was "What time is it? Man, I don't even know what day it is."

Ken had kept on plugging away and winding his watch. He was pretty happy with the way his life went. Every now and then someone in the dorm would tell him about an epiphanous psychedelic experience or how good sex was on Quaaludes. And Ken would wonder whether he wasn't wasting his life in the lab. But the thought would pass quickly. He met Laura during his junior year. She was soon persuaded to wear an engagement ring, even though she maintained that it didn't go with her wardrobe of denim skirts and peasant blouses. Laura taught art in a series of private schools while Ken got through medical school and his residency. He had always thought they'd eventually move to the suburbs, but Laura could never bring herself to learn to drive. So they settled on a brownstone in Park Slope. Ken shared space on Central Park West and his practice did well. And dermatology was an easy specialty to live with, with regular hours and a minimal involvement with death.

What Ken liked about medicine was that everyone was on the same side. He and his patients were joined in the search for the correct diagnosis and treatment, searching for the ultimate truth. It wasn't like law, where you chose a side and did battle with each other. Lawyers could go over to the other side on a moment's notice, but a doctor was always on the right side. Ken liked that. And even though dermatology was sometimes considered more of a punch line than a medical specialty, Ken found it stimulating.

The medical capitalist stuff had started with a simple tax shelter deal that his accountant had cut him in on—a shopping center in Memphis. It did so well that he couldn't resist going in on the next one. And the next. He started skimming his medical journals and reading Medical Economics from cover to cover.

Then intrusive thoughts started occurring to him while he was examining his patients. Thoughts of capital gains treatment and depreciation. Ken found himself agonizing more over tax reform than he ever had over melanoma. He watched colleagues give up the practice of medicine entirely, move to Taos, and have computer terminals installed in their hot tubs so they could keep an eye on the market while they soaked. He didn't want that to happen to him. He kept telling himself that he'd go cold turkey. Soon. When he had made just a bit more money. Just one more deal.

Was real-estate investment the drug of the eighties? Ken wondered. Had he led such a clean life up until now, staying away from cocaine, never cheating on Laura, just to be haunted by the constant craving for a quick fix of sheltered income? It was becoming a major concern. So when Nina accused him at the dinner table of being a medical capitalist, she hit a nerve.

Don't get defensive, Ken told himself. Getting defensive around Nina was like cutting yourself while shaving in a shark tank. He became determinedly conciliatory. "No big deal. If I can't sublet, I can't. But if the price is below market, I can always flip. It's at least worth looking into."

"No harm in looking," Ida said. "But I don't know when that foreign corporation is going to put the apartment on the market. They might want to do some work on it first."

"Is it really a mess?" asked Laura.

"It's not great," her mother replied. "Ever since the building converted, you can imagine that Mrs. Gross had an impossible time getting any work done when it was needed. Rabinowitz couldn't wait for her to die or move into a nursing home. And it didn't get any better after West Estates bought it. She had to go after them to paint and make even the most basic repairs. But the one thing they were completely fastidious about was exterminating."

"What do you mean?" Nina asked.

"They didn't use the regular building exterminator. They used their own guy. And according to Mrs. Gross he came frequently and was very good. Hers was the only apartment in the building where a roach was never seen. I always meant to try that exterminator, but I never got around to it."

"Now, what do you think this means?" said Nina. "Steve also said that the only problem Mrs. Kahn didn't have was cockroaches."

"That is strange," said Ida.

"Do you think the major shareholder of this corporation has a cockroach fetish?" said Nina.

"Maybe exterminating is a big thing in the Netherlands Antilles," said Laura. "You know, in these tropical places even the fanciest high-rises have huge bugs."

"Just like Manhattan," Nina said.

"Look, Laura, these people don't actually live in the Netherlands Antilles. They just incorporate there for tax purposes." Ken sounded impatient.

Ida shook her head. "I doubt if the shareholders of West Estates even know if their New York apartments are being exterminated. If anyone has a cockroach fetish, it's probably Myron Kaplan."

"Who's he?"

"West Estate's New York attorney and unofficial managing agent."

"Who probably has a brother-in-law who's an exterminator," said Nina.

"I have an idea," said Ken, who still sounded impatient. "Call Myron Kaplan and find out the name of his brother-in-law the exterminator. Why not get rid of your cockroaches if you can? Get the whole building to use him."

"Yeah, Ma," said Nina. You could get into the Home section of the *Times*—the only building on the Upper West Side that's free of cockroach infestation."

"And while you're at it," said Ken, "ask Myron Kaplan if the apartment is up for sale and when we could see it."

Nina turned to her mother. "He's smooth, isn't he? Manipulating with a light touch. I don't know what happened to all that boyish earnestness the young Dr. Rubin used to have."

"And you, Nina," Ken continued, "should give your friend Steve a call. Find out the address of Mrs. Kahn's apartment. Let's look at both places. Maybe I can pick up the two of them cheap."

"That's what I like," said Nina. "A man who can talk about real estate as though he's talking about dry goods. Very erotic."

That set Laura off. "Is that what you're finding erotic these days? Whatever happened to black men who took you to after-hours clubs with boxes of Kleenex on the bar?"

"For chrissakes, Laura. My mother happens to be sitting at this table."

"It's okay," Ida said. "I know about the black men and the after-hours bars. But I don't understand about the Kleenex."

"In those days," Nina explained, "the kind of people who went to after-hours clubs had runny noses from snorting too much coke. That was before they started smoking it."

Ida looked horrified. "Spare me," she said.

"Don't worry, Ma. My nose remained intact. You know I've always managed to confine my addictions to Chinese food."

"Can we get back on point here?" said Ken. "The way this family's conversations wander off, it's amazing anyone ever gets anything done."

Nina felt that "wander off" was a mischaracterization. She considered conversation a contemporary art form and the Fischmans particularly talented. "Think of how lucky you are," she told Ken. "You could have married into a family with no oral tradition. Who just grunted and passed the mashed potatoes. Instead you get treated to lively dinner conversation.

Try thinking of us as chroniclers of the human spirit instead of a bunch of yentas."

"You must have a little compassion for the man," Ida said to Nina. "I don't think he grew up around chroniclers of the human spirit."

"No, I guess he didn't," Nina agreed. "Not with a mother and two sisters who spend their lives at the manicurist. It's hard to chronicle the human spirit when the woman who's wrapping your nails doesn't speak English."

Ken noticed that Nina was getting a laugh out of Laura. "You know, you're a turncoat," he said to his wife. She shrugged. He turned back to Nina and Ida. "Do me a favor. Make those calls as soon as possible."

"He's hot to trot," Nina said to her mother. "Maybe we should hold out for a finder's fee."

"And don't forget to find out the name of that exterminator," said Laura. "It would be so much nicer for the children if you got rid of the roaches in your apartment. It upsets them."

"Tough," said Nina. "Seeing a few roaches is good for them. They're too sheltered. I don't want my niece and nephew to grow up to be wimps."

"We'll take them to the cockroach zoo twice a year," said Ken. "We promise. Listen, Ida. While you're at it, it wouldn't hurt if you could feel the board out on whether I have a shot at getting permission to sublet."

"There's a board meeting next Thursday," Ida said. "I'll feel them out. I promise."

5

IDA GLANCED AROUND THE ROOM at the other board members. Her building had a five-person board. Four of the persons wore navy blue suits. Ida, the fifth person, wore purple. The board was discussing potential investments. The building reserve fund had been invested in short-term paper that was about to come due, and there was a great deal of disagreement about where to invest next.

"Can't we do something about the lobby this time?" asked Bo Marsh. Marsh was always suggesting redecorating the lobby. He occupied the homosexual seat on the board, and his redecoration fetish had become a standing joke.

Ida studied the four men. They were almost indistinguishable from one another, except for Bo's mustache. It was one of those extremely well trimmed ones that served as an acceptable substitute for a gay pride button in the corporate world.

"I see pin spots," said Marsh. "With some decent art on the walls. Maybe with an important piece of sculpture on a marble plinth to draw your eyes away from the freight elevator."

Bob Carroll rolled his eyes. "Knowing you, you'll blow the whole reserve fund on the plinth. We're reinvesting the entire amount, and that's that." Carroll was a one-man frivolity vigilante committee. At the last meeting he had vetoed the idea of an air conditioner for the board room. Ida had taken a dislike to him the first time she met him. He had been with his wife who was in the unfortunate position of being named Carol Carroll. It was the way he introduced her that pissed Ida off. "This is my wife, Carol Carroll," with a big nasty laugh while Mrs. Carroll squirmed with embarrassment. In a way that let you know he had forced the poor woman to change her name when they got married because he found it amusing. He was cheap and nasty.

Marsh and Carroll represented the two board extremes. In the center, along with Ida, were Mark Cohen and Mark Sadow. Ida found the Marks less colorful but easier to deal with than Marsh and Carroll. Ida referred to the Marks and herself as the Jewish vote. The Jews spent a lot of time mediating between the two Christians.

All of the men had professions that were expected of board members in a West End Avenue co-op. Two of them were bankers. Marsh was an investment banker for a small but well-known firm. Cohen worked for the New York branch of a Japanese bank. Carroll was a litigator for a large Wall Street law firm. He displayed the classic litigator's tic, nervously glancing at his watch every two minutes. Sadow was an architect. His job was to come up with a reason to justify vetoing everyone's alteration plans.

Over the years the job of being a member of the board had become easier. For the first few years following the building's conversion, the board had been like an armed camp. The shareholders, still new to their status, and the non-purchasing tenants had all assumed that the board was simply the latest incarnation of their landlord and had hated it accordingly. As the sponsor slowly lost control of the board, feelings of suspicion subsided. During the first year, the converter held four seats; during the second year he held three. Ida was chosen to replace him as the third seat, the swing vote. Therefore, she was regarded as somewhat of a folk heroine in the building. The Marks had been on the board since the second year. Marsh and Carroll were more recent additions.

Ida tired of listening to the battle of the lobby. Her attention wandered. It wasn't the first time. In fact, it wasn't the first time in the past ten minutes. This time it wandered to the men's wrists. Watches could be very revealing. Marsh wore a handsome moon-phase watch with a face that curved around his wrist. Extremely fashionable, a perfect watch for a gay investment banker. Carroll wore an inexpensive, nondescript Seiko, which he consulted every other minute. The Marks wore Rolexes at opposite ends of the price scale. Sadow's was gold and huge, while Cohen's was humble and stainless steel. Apparently Cohen's Japanese bank did not insist upon his wearing a Japanese watch. Ida knew that he drove a Japanese car. Sadow drove a Ferrari. He was the only person Ida had ever heard of who owned one. It fit with the watch. And yet he was only an architect, and not a very well-known one at that, Ida thought to herself.

She reined her attention back in. The meeting was winding down and she had promised Ken to feel out the board about subletting. Of course, she knew that Ken's concern was premature. He hadn't even looked at Mrs. Gross's apartment yet. But it never hurt to pave the way. "I've been thinking about subletting," Ida said.

"Where are you off to now?" said Bo, with more than a hint of jealousy. Bo loved to travel, but couldn't get away often enough to suit him. Ida, on the other hand, had really been getting around lately, making up for all those decades in the Bronx. She had to lay off, though. Her native artifact display area was getting overcrowded.

"I haven't been thinking about subletting my apartment.

I've been thinking about our subletting policy in general. About how strict we've been in granting permission."

"I think it's a sound policy," said Bob Carroll, glancing nervously at his watch. "If people want to sublet, let them buy a condo." Condo boards typically had less of a strangle-hold on the owners. It was Ida's private theory that this was the reason co-ops instead of condos were the popular form of ownership in New York. It was easier to ruin your neighbor's life.

"I think it's unreasonable—I always have," said Mark Cohen. They all ignored him, since he took the position clearly out of self-interest. It was well known that Cohen lived in constant fear of being temporarily transferred to Tokyo.

"I don't want a lot of weird subtenants running around the building," said Mark Sadow. "For example, take the apartment on top of me. The one where that old lady named Gross just died. I assume it will be sold soon. With a reputation for being a building with a lax subletting policy, God knows who'll buy that apartment. Probably some investor and then I'll have a different set of lunatic subtenants jumping on my head every year."

"Maybe we should be deciding on a case-by-case basis," Cohen suggested, "instead of approaching every request with the assumption that we're going to deny it."

"I agree," said Marsh. While Kaplan worried about two years in Tokyo, Marsh fantasized about a leave of absence in Mykonos.

"I strongly disagree," said Carroll.

The lines were clearly drawn—two for, two against. Ida was the swing vote. She could probably push the board into granting Ken permission to sublet if he bought Mrs. Gross's apartment.

Well, she'd tell Ken it was worth looking into. And she'd give Myron Kaplan a call to see when it would be going on the market. Maybe Ken could take a look at it before it was actually listed. She'd go with him, of course. No one would pass up such a preview. Looking at vacant apartments was becoming everyone's favorite hobby. Not because they were looking to buy, but just out of curiosity. It had become the major Sunday afternoon preoccupation for the latest generation of affluent New Yorkers. What the tailgate picnic must have been to their parents.

"Let's discuss this further when we actually have a request before us," said Sadow. "Besides, it's getting close to ten o'clock."

"Ten o'clock" was a euphemism for "L.A. Law." The board meeting, which traditionally took place on Thursday, always broke in time for "L.A. Law." Even though everyone owned a VCR, it was somehow important to see the show immediately. Seeing it a day late was pointless. Like reading the *Times* at night. You just couldn't keep up with Friday morning office conversation. Even Ida, who had no office conversation to keep up with, felt this way. So no sooner were the words ten o'clock out of Sadow's mouth than the meeting broke up.

6

THE NEXT DAY Ida phoned Myron Kaplan. She didn't actually get to talk to him, of course. Talking to lawyers was for paying customers. But his secretary was very pleasant and cooperative. Her name was Louise. She was one of those old-fashioned types. One of those legal secretaries who spoke with such calm authority that you just knew they'd been practicing without a license all these years. Louise was only too happy to set up a viewing of Mrs. Gross's apartment. The client was anxious to sell, she said. Although some renovations were planned, they'd be willing to negotiate an "as is" sale. Louise arranged for the real-estate agent to meet Ken and Ida at the apartment on Saturday.

The agent was a bit late on Saturday, and there was some fumbling about with the keys, but she eventually let them in. The apartment had been given only the merest once-over. It was not even what they called in the trade "broom clean." Patricia White, the agent, looked stricken when they first walked through. But she gained her composure quickly and started using the word *potential* a lot. While Ken examined the rooms, Ida examined the agent. Women like Patricia White always astounded Ida. She found it hard to believe that she and this creature were both *Homo sapiens*. They bore so little resemblance to each other. Patricia White had a high center of gravity. She wore three-inch heels and was extremely long-stemmed. Ida was more of a dachshund. White's crotch seemed to be level with Ida's clavicle. And she was so narrow and small-boned that Ida was afraid she'd break. She could barely watch her totter around on those heels. It looked dangerous.

"The schools in the area," White was saying to Ken, "are some of the best in the city. There's Trinity and Collegiate. Even the public school has gotten very good, from what I hear."

"Well, I sort of figure the kids will go to Dalton. Even if it means going across the park every day," Ken said.

"I didn't hear you say Dalton, did I?" Ida scurried across the room. "Not for my grandchildren."

"Dalton's one of the best," said White.

Ida's friend Rose had a grandchild who went to Dalton. Rose was always complaining about the rarefied atmosphere of the place. She said they put the children's finger paintings in chrome frames and the goldfish in recessed tanks built into the wall. And that her grandson spoke with such pretentious lockjaw that she didn't understand what he was saying. Matthew was like her cousin Stanley, Rose said. Stanley's mother never learned English and by the time he was bar mitzvahed he had forgotten all his Yiddish. He couldn't talk to his own mother. It was heartbreaking, Rose said, and now it had happened to her in a way. She hoped it wouldn't happen to Ida. Push for the public schools, Rose told her.

"I don't want my grandchildren going to school with only white kids," Ida said.

"Diana Ross's three daughters go there," White offered.

Ida shook her head. "They don't count." She wasn't a big *People* magazine reader, but she distinctly remembered that the daughters' last name was something like Silverberg. One of them was named Chudney, but being named after a condiment, even a misspelled one, did not exempt you from white-kid status. She appealed to Ken. "Besides, it costs a fortune."

"That's for sure." Ken thought about a guy he had met at a party recently who sent his kid to Dalton. The guy had said it cost him two grand that year to send her there. Ken had said that two grand sounded cheap for tuition. The guy laughed at him as he explained that it cost two grand to send her there, to get her there by taxi service. Carfare was two grand, tuition was extra. Ken wasn't sure he wanted his kid hanging around with the offspring of people who bragged about carfare at parties.

"Will you excuse us for a moment?" Ken asked the broker.

"Take your time." Patricia White leaned against a windowsill and slipped out of her high heels.

Ken took Ida into the kitchen. "Let me ask you something," he said. "Did we or did we not just have an argument about where to send the kids to school in a neighborhood that we both know I'm not even moving into?"

Ida was poking around in the kitchen cabinets, on to a new topic. "I want you to look at these cabinets," she said.

"They're ugly," said Ken.

"Of course they're ugly. They're left over from the Second World War." The kitchen cabinets were wood and had been painted so many times that the doors had swollen to unclosable proportions.

"I see granite countertops." Ken swept his hand grandly. "With a work island here. Black granite with a lot of stainless steel. Maybe gray Formica cabinets. And that same tile we have on our kitchen floor, but in gray instead of terra-cotta."

"Ken, how do you know what tile you have in your kitchen? I've never seen you in it."

"Home design is a big thing with husbands these days. It's up there with parenting."

"In my day if a man so much as admitted he knew what color his kitchen floor tile was, his status as a heterosexual became suspect. Anyway, aside from being ugly, what else is noticeable about these cabinets?"

"I give up. I can't see beyond their glaring unsightliness."

"No trace of roaches. No eggs, no corpses, no feces."

"Maybe that's because the place was recently cleaned."

"But it wasn't cleaned really well. Look, the doors are still covered with fingerprints. Here's a sticky patch about the size and shape of the bottom of a Log Cabin maple syrup bottle. And there are still tiny hills of crumbs in all the corners. Whoever cleaned did a very superficial job. Not thorough enough to remove all traces of roach remains. But there are traces of a fine white powder, which must be what they're using to kill the roaches."

Ida could tell that Ken wasn't listening. Well, what could she expect? What did he know from roaches? They clearly weren't a major theme in his life. Ida didn't even know if Ken and Laura had a roach problem. It wasn't something Laura discussed with her. It was funny how different her daughters were about those kinds of things. If something was unpleasant or unattractive, Laura would quietly hide it, while Nina would drag it out for detailed inspection.

Ida's attitude toward roaches was a complex one. It was true that they were the bane of her existence and had been for decades. She had spent her entire life wrapping everything up in plastic bags. But roaches also symbolized something unique about New York. Rich people and poor people had them. They were the great equalizer, like the subway system. Ida enjoyed seeing all types packed in, shoulder to shoulder, on the subway. It provided exposure, as opposed to towns like Los Angeles where rich people rode around in air-conditioned cars with the windows rolled up and poor people waited on bus-stop benches that advertised funeral parlors.

And all the hardships that New Yorkers endured gave them more opportunity for feelings of accomplishment. Every time Ida got a seat on the subway her spirit soared. It made her feel that life was going her way. That she had achieved something, albeit small, that day. You never got to experience this sense of triumph out of town. Ida also believed that the more stimulation people were exposed to, the more complex they became. Ida felt understimulated in other places, as if the world had lost a dimension. The horizon always seemed low, and an almost silent hum replaced the street noise she was used to, as if a big fan were running in the background.

But it was the people out of town that really terrified her. Their eyes stared straight ahead. In New York, she could tell how smart a person was by the number of quick little movements his eyes made. She felt sorry for those people whose eyes didn't move. They were usually exhausted or drug addicts or retarded. But out of town, even the high-functioning people didn't move their eyes. The bank managers, the traffic cops, the restaurant hostesses, all stared straight ahead. Ida only trusted shifty-eyed people. Sometimes a slight but intelligent squint could compensate for eye darting, but something had to be going on up there.

And then there was the clothing issue. New Yorkers dressed in intelligent though depressing colors. Greige, taupe, mushroom, elephant. Call it what you would, the predominant color in most New York wardrobes was the shade of second-day street slush. You'd never catch a New Yorker in one of those sherbet colors they wore out of town. Peach, lemon, melon, lime. Most New Yorkers wouldn't even eat sherbet, much less wear it. Nina felt the same way. She said that her wardrobe, which usually seemed perfectly normal, suddenly turned weird whenever it spent time in a suitcase. By the time it was unpacked out of town, it made Nina look like the sister from another planet.

And then there was the locomotion issue. Not that Ida was one of those New York women who had never learned to drive. Even though the Fischmans had never made it to the suburbs, they had managed to own a series of old bombs for Sunday expeditions. But Ida's primary means of locomotion was walking. She felt that she derived her energy from the connection her feet made with concrete. Driving made her feel powerless, as if the gas pedal had severed the connection between her and her energy source. And there was no place like New York for walking. She had a fancy pair of New Balance shoes with a reflecting patch on their back. Just in case she was ever jogging at night on a country road.

So New York was still pretty much New York. You could walk, ride the subway, and wear gray. But Ida didn't know what to make of the recent influx of out-of-towners who seemed to be taking over the city. There were Texas blondes in white fur coats living on streets that her parents had moved away from sixty years ago. And all those gay men, so fair-haired and angelic and all dressed alike. Like a huge Boy Scout troop from Minnesota that had been released in town. It was nice that at least some people had a look of vulnerability in New York. Everyone else looked so tough. Like survivors. Like cockroaches.

Ida continued her survey of what used to be Mrs. Gross's kitchen. It wasn't really large enough to be called an eat-in, although maybe you could sneak a tiny table into a corner. And it really was a shambles. Not the kitchen an out-of-towner would imagine in an apartment that had been priced at $650,000. But New Yorkers took a perverse pride in paying exorbitant sums for tiny, decayed spaces. It made them feel more sophisticated, more European.

Patricia White tottered in on her three-inch heels. "It has a lot of potential, don't you think?" the agent chirped.

Ida watched her totter. She felt a flicker of a familiar

emotion. A mixture of pity, contempt, and jealousy. White was obviously a divorcée who had spent her married life in someplace like Greenwich. It was clear that she had been pampered and was nervous in her new role as a woman making a living. A role Ida had been born into. Ida felt sorry for her, but couldn't help thinking what a silly woman she was. Even if life was tough and White had some bad breaks—her husband ran out on her, screwed her on the alimony, her kids only called once a month—she could at least make her life easier by wearing shoes she could walk in. Then the third emotion kicked in, the one Ida felt most uncomfortable about. She was jealous of this pathetic creature. Of the emaciated figure White struggled so hard to maintain. Of her caved-in chest. Of her bleached moussed hair. Of her torturous shoes. And of her six-hundred-dollar suit. Images of White in her past life flashed into Ida's mind. She saw her in one of those golf skirts at the country club eating a tomato stuffed with crabmeat. In a suburban branch of Saks getting her husband's shirts monogrammed. She saw Mr. and Mrs. White in a big sedan, driving home after a party, playfully arguing about how many scotches Mr. White had drunk. Leo had strictly been a seltzer drinker.

If she could do it all over again and had a choice this time, which way would she go? she wondered. Would she go back to the Hunter College cafeteria and the Young People's Socialist League and teaching forty-five kids in a class? And all those cockroaches, a never-ending procession? Or would she choose to put on the high heels, suffer a bunion or two, and trade in the roaches for exquisite floral arrangements, engraved invitations, and silk blouses? And all that went with it. Dependence, timidity, deference. The truth was that it was a hard choice. Ida wished she could say that she wouldn't change a minute of her life. That she was a fighter and enjoyed all the struggles she had been through. The union organizing, the working motherhood, the years of psycho-analysis. That if she had been one of those coddled creatures, she would have ended up in the bin. But in all honesty, who really knew? Maybe she would have loved it. Taken to golf and charity luncheons like a duck to water. Enjoyed pampering her man and dressing her little girls in velvet and lace.

Instead, she had Laura, the mystery child. Everyone had wondered where this kid came from. With a background like hers, how come she gave tea parties for her dolls complete with fish forks? Leo could never figure Laura out. He didn't know what a fish fork was. It didn't make sense to him that his six-year-old daughter knew. Ida would shrug her shoulders, but she had to admit that a small piece of herself was in that child. The piece that thought it wouldn't be so awful to have been Patricia White.

At the moment, Patricia White seemed less than ecstatic. She shifted from foot to foot, as if even the tiny amount of weight her frame contained was too much to bear. She kept smiling, though. Ken asked her about the other apartment, the one that Mrs. Kahn had died in. He took her by surprise. She seemed disoriented. "How did you know about that?"

"Just a coincidence," said Ken. "But it sounds similar to this one and I thought it would be worth looking at."

"As a matter of fact, I showed it to someone earlier today."

"Do you still have the keys on you?"

"Yes."

"Do you think we could take a look at it now?"

"I don't see why not. It's only a few blocks away."

Ida looked doubtfully at White's shoes. "Maybe we should take a cab," she said. It was practically against her religion to take taxis, especially since she got half-fare privileges on public transportation for being a senior citizen. But if ever it was appropriate, now was the time. She just couldn't bear watching this poor creature hobble up West End Avenue.

They did take a cab, and then there was more fumbling with keys, but once they got inside, Ida saw that Kahn's apartment was spectacular. Gross's apartment had been impressive, with oversized rooms and a sliver of a river view. But Kahn's was really something. It was on the top floor, and both the living room and the master bedroom had unobstructed views of the Hudson River. A dining room of grand proportions had oak-paneled walls and French doors. A long hall led to two more bedrooms, two bathrooms, and a maid's room. The kitchen was huge, and there was a breakfast room off one end.

It was wild, thought Ida as she poked around the kitchen, to imagine some little old lady in a tattered nightgown grandly sweeping up and down these halls. And probably paying less in controlled rent than it would have cost her to move to a studio apartment in Queens. The old lady must have been a prisoner of rent control.

Ida could see why these landlords got venomous at the mention of rent regulation. But with the way New York real-estate values had been going, if rents were allowed to climb to market, the result would be a city filled with young bankers while the native New Yorkers would all be packed up and shipped off to live on large rural compounds. All those lower-middle-class ethnics who once tended their roses in Carroll Gardens or clacked their mah-jongg tiles on the slopes of Riverdale would find themselves shivering in the North Dakota winter. Rent deregulation was too reminiscent of the Final Solution. But, on the other hand, Ida thought, keeping some old lady trapped in a once-grand apartment that she couldn't keep up was ridiculous. Everything about the place needed repairs. It must have been depressing for Mrs. Kahn.

Ida opened a kitchen cabinet and did a quick roach scan. The cabinets had the same roachless quality as the ones in the Gross apartment, with the same traces of white powder. She was about to call Ken in from the dining room, but she decided not to bother. He hadn't seemed interested, and if there was one thing Ida had, it was a sense of audience. She would call Nina as soon as she got home. Nina had a keen interest in roach eradication and was always looking for new methods.

7

NINA WAS SPENDING A TYPICAL SATURDAY in her apartment, obsessing about what to do first, when her mother called. Her house needed cleaning, the clothes to be dry cleaned lay in piles, the refrigerator was empty, and a half-written brief sat on her dining room table. There were four unanswered messages on her phone machine, and she hadn't even looked at the cartoons in that week's *New Yorker*. She hadn't gotten to exercise class all week, and Grant had said something about some obscure film that they had to see that day before it disappeared forever. Nina somehow luxuriated in all this overextension. It made her feel connected, even though it was all a pain in the ass. And even if she just sat on the couch all day, accomplishing nothing, she was still a woman with things to do. Never again would she have that "nothing to do" feeling that used to strike her as she sat in the college dorm on rainy Sundays. Nina collected things to do.

Now she scanned the *New Yorker* as she listened to her mother talk about cockroaches. Ida was going on and on about how remarkably roach-free the old ladies' apartments had been. New Yorkers spent so much time on their cockroach problem, Nina thought. What did out-of-towners do with all that time? Not to mention the bank lines, subway rides, and weekly psychotherapy sessions they didn't have to go through. They probably finished their attics or something. She often wondered the same thing about women who didn't have a weight problem. If she added up all the time and money she'd spent on that during her life, she could probably have gotten her pilot's license about ten times over.

As her mother went on, a cockroach marched across Nina's kitchen counter, as if for illustrative purposes. She mentally added exterminating to her to-do list. "What did it look like the exterminator was using?" she asked her mother. "Did you see roach traps or powder or anything?"

"Powder. Little piles of a fine white powder in the corners of the kitchen cabinets. I think I saw traces in the other rooms, too, but I wasn't sure."

"Ma, we should get the name of this exterminator. I would definitely use him. I'm not as tormented by roaches as you are, but I could live without them."

"I don't know how I would feel about having powder spread all over my apartment. It could be somewhat unsightly."

"What's a little powder?" Nina said. "Haven't you become the fancy Manhattan lady. The woman who lived with a beach chair in the living room."

Ida had had a beach chair in the living room only briefly, years ago, although her decorating scheme had never been exactly *House & Garden*. She had started her marriage off with Danish Modern. Back then Ida had a deep philosophical and political commitment to modern furniture. Its spare lines and simple materials represented twentieth-century egalitarianism. Having a modern living room was the progressive thing to do. Wasn't Scandinavia a haven of socialized medicine? Traditional furniture, the ornately carved overstuffed variety, was considered reactionary. It was what Ida's parents, who were still living in the nineteenth century, had. To Ida, brocade couches meant Orthodox Judaism and all that went with it—narrow-mindedness, repression of women, and capitalism. Teak was the wood of enlightenment.

As the years went by and the furniture began to wear out, there was no money to replace it. Ida went through several phases. For a while she refused to buy anything else, hoping she'd be able to afford replacements soon. The beach chair was a relic of this era. Then she started to buy cheap at Foamland like the other wives in the neighborhood. But the stuff seemed to last only a matter of months. So she switched to the secondhand route, buying up furniture every time someone in the building died. Because of the unpredictability of the supply, Ida had a tendency to be a hoarder. At one point, she owned three couches.

Nina's decorating scheme had also gone through many transitions, all typical of her subculture. And since she never threw anything out, anyone with a halfway decent sociological eye could walk through her apartment and spot artifacts from each year of the second half of the twentieth century. At the moment you could find a spider plant from 1971, an earring rack from 1966, a Patty Playpal from 1957, a Breuer chair from 1977, a Tizio lamp from 1984, and a Tensor lamp from 1964.

Her seashell collection was timeless, however. You couldn't look at a chambered nautilus the way you could look at a lamp and tell whether it was from 1964 or 1984. Nina had started collecting shells in the fourth grade and never stopped. She felt comfortable with them because they were uniformly beautiful. There was no such thing as an ugly seashell. She didn't always trust her own taste, which was never as developed as Laura's, but with shells she could make no mistakes. For a while Nina had switched to houseplants, but they proved to be trickier. There were ugly houseplants, like snake plants growing in ceramic frogs and stringy philodendrons potted in coffee cans.

Everyone loved seashells. Collecting shells wasn't a nerdy hobby, like collecting stamps or coins. The other girls in her class thought they were neat because they were pretty and feminine. Ida approved of them in a way that she would never approve of Barbie's wardrobe. They were intellectual. And Leo approved of them because of their inherent intellectuality and also because they were cheaper than Barbie's wardrobe and reinforced no bourgeois stereotypes. Their primitivism appealed to him, and they could be universally appreciated by all classes. Laura liked them but wasn't about to switch over and stop expanding her Barbie's wardrobe. Nina was especially fond of them because they reminded her of water. Like many chubby kids, Nina felt most comfortable when she was submerged. It was in the water that her athletic abilities blossomed. Terror from years of being chosen last for schoolyard teams would evaporate at summer camp where she would head up the swimming relay races. Nina considered herself a water mammal.

So she schlepped the shells around with her for decades. Throwing out a seashell was unimaginable. And now scattered throughout her apartment were ruffled clams, spotted cowries, lacy murexes, volutes, scallops, whelks, conchs, and a few valuable wentletraps.

She was less fond of cockroaches, although she had a healthy collection of those, too. She didn't mind them as much as some people did. The kids who grew up in the suburbs were especially squeamish. Nina was hardened from a lifetime of exposure. Screaming and carrying on was a sign of weakness to her. She could casually squash a roach with a tissue or even her bare hand without flinching.

Recently Nina had vowed to hire an exterminator. The one provided by the building did little more than give a lackadaisical squirt every third Thursday. Fueling her desire was the fact that she was in the midst of her spring cleaning. "Spring cleaning" was an overstatement. Her campaign so far had consisted of little more than her annual refrigerator defrost. She usually let the freezer get to the point where you could slide only a Popsicle in and out. Last week she had also cleaned the oven, since it had set off the smoke detector when she tried to use it. Nina was on a domestic roll.

"Really, Ma, what's a little white powder?" Nina repeated. "Maybe you don't truly want to get rid of your cockroaches. In some neurotic way you're attached to them."

"My own form of success anxiety, perhaps. But don't overlook the invasion-rape theory. The thought of a strange man invading my cabinets has a phallic content that I might find threatening."

"You're still hopelessly mired in all that antiquated Freudian stuff. When are you going to drop your psychoanalyst and move on to a shrink with a more enlightened approach? Even psychoanalysts don't go to psychoanalysts anymore."

"Well, actually, I've been talking about terminating."

"Ma, you've been talking about terminating since Nixon started talking about resigning."

"That's the pot calling the kettle black."

"I've only been talking about terminating for a mere three, maybe four years." Nina was so used to therapy that she couldn't imagine herself without it. It was like getting her hair cut. If she didn't go, she'd get fuzzy. "Anyway, how would we go about getting the name of this exterminator?"

"I suppose I could call Myron Kaplan again. His secretary put us in touch with the broker pretty quickly. Maybe she'd do the same with the exterminator. I'll call the office on Monday. How's that?"

"Great," said Nina. "Maybe he'll give us a joint session."

8

"**I**T'S SOME LADY NAMED FISCHMAN." Myron Kaplan's secretary spoke through the intercom.

"Who the hell is she?" he snapped back.

"She's on the board in one of the West Estates buildings. She wants to know the name of the exterminator that West Estates uses."

"How the hell should I know that? Get rid of her."

"Myron, I've been getting rid of people for you for seventeen years now, haven't I?"

"Yeah."

"And doing a good job of it, too."

"Yes, you have, Louise."

"Well, by this time I can tell who I can get rid of and who I can't. Mrs. Fischman I can't get rid of. You're going to have to do that yourself. She's called three times already. Push oh-four, please."

Myron Kaplan pushed 04, but not without rolling his eyes. His gesture was instantly recognizable. An anthropological treatise on eye rolling in the twentieth-century American male would note that it was done immediately preceding an act of deference to an American female. Husbands did it while producing American Express cards. Little boys did it while extending their hands for holding in schoolyard lines. And lawyers did it while allowing their secretaries to dictate what calls they would take.

"Hello." If Myron Kaplan had been a young associate, he would have answered the phone by saying "Myron Kaplan" instead of "hello." But then his name wouldn't have been Myron Kaplan. If he'd been a young associate, his name would have been Steven Kaplan or Mark Kaplan. Myron Kaplan wasn't anyone's associate. And he wasn't young. He had gone to law school in the days when speedwriting was still a recommended course. So he answered his phone with a curt "hello" or, on days when he felt particularly cranky, a simple "yah?"

"Good morning, Mr. Kaplan. Thank you for taking my call. This is Ida Fischman, a member of the board of directors at three-nineteen West End Avenue. Your client, West Estates, owns apartment seven-A. I believe we've spoken before."

Myron Kaplan had a dim recollection of some lady calling him up to hock him about replacement windows in that building. Maybe it had been Ida Fischman. "What can I do for you?"

"If you recall, your client independently contracted for the services of an exterminator for apartment seven-A."

"Yah?" Myron Kaplan was starting to get cranky. He was wary of old ladies who tried to sound like lawyers. But they weren't as bad as old ladies who actually were lawyers. They were the worst. He had never encountered one who failed to remind him of Bella Abzug.

"I'd like to know the name of your exterminator."

"My exterminator? I don't have an exterminator. I don't need one. I live on Long Island. We don't have roaches there."

"Your client's exterminator, then."

"How should I know the name of my client's exterminator? Do I know the name of my client's cleaning lady? Or barber? Or garage mechanic?"

"Mr. Kaplan, your client is a Netherlands Antilles corporation. It's doubtful whether your client has a cleaning lady or a barber or a garage mechanic. You are the managing agent of record for West Estates, N. V. If I need a piece of information regarding your client, I have no one other than yourself to contact."

"All right, I'll tell my girl to find out the name of the exterminator. She'll get back to you." Myron Kaplan hit the intercom. Ida heard him say "Louise, get Mrs. Fischman's phone number." The phone clicked and she was on the line with Louise.

She gave Louise her phone number. This was hopeless, she thought. Maybe Nina could do better. She decided to try her daughter in the office, even though at this hour she might still be in court. She was there, though.

"Sorry to bother you at the office, dear."

"It's better than bothering me at home."

"Well, you leave me no choice. You don't answer your phone at night anymore. All I get is the machine."

Nina sighed. It was true. Talking on the phone used to be a joy. When she was a kid and would hear her mother say "Nina, it's for you," her heart would soar. In college, she and her roommates would get hold of corporate credit card numbers so that they could call friends in California and Michigan. It was criminal, but free phone conversations seemed worth it at the time. In law school, she would pray to the phone, hoping to hear from various men who had once given her a vague indication that they might communicate with her telephonically. It used to be an instrument of intrigue, mystery, drama, and erotica. Now she worked long days. Her mornings were spent in court trying to persuade rabidly furious landlords not to evict her clients. Her afternoons and early evenings were spent on the telephone with these creatures' attorneys trying to work out deals preventing these evictions. She often spent seven hours a day on the phone, much of it with a raised voice. The phone was no longer an instrument of joy.

"Ma, I'm on the phone all day long," she said. "Asking me to answer my phone at night is like expecting a hooker to make love to her husband after turning twenty tricks that day."

"I never thought about that," Ida said. "What do hookers do about their marital sex lives?"

"I think some of them are lesbians. And a lot of them have a pimp with such a large stable that they only have to screw him once in a while. Like Mormons or Arabs. Is that why you called? To check up on the home life of our prostitute population?"

"I just wanted to let you know that I spoke with Myron Kaplan, that lawyer for the Netherlands Antilles corporation that owns Mrs. Gross's apartment. And he was the most extraordinarily rude person. I couldn't believe he was really a lawyer. I thought maybe you could check and see whether he's actually admitted to practice law."

Nina could easily have looked him up in Martindale Hubbell, the lawyers' directory and gossipmonger's bible. But she knew what she'd find. First she'd find about thirty-five Myron Kaplans. Then she'd find a Myron Kaplan at the address Ida had given her. And he would have gone to New York Law School and graduated in 1938. His specialty would be collection work. Nina was sure he was rude and horrible and probably a cheap crook and worthy of disbarment. But she was just as sure he was admitted to practice law in the state of New York. "You're more naive than I thought," she told her mother. "Since when does being a lawyer make you a decent human being?"

"I suppose I am naive."

"You're naive when it's convenient. It's a sensible attitude."

"Well, I'm not naive enough to believe that Myron Kaplan is actually going to bother to give me the name of that exterminator. I know when I'm getting brushed off. And this guy made me feel like a flea."

"Okay, do this. Call him a couple of times. Write to him on the co-op board's stationery. If that doesn't work, I'll intervene in your behalf as your attorney. Eventually we'll get the name of the exterminator."

"Thank you, dear."

"Anytime, Mother." Could she desert her now, when the Fischman Battle of the Roaches was about to near a dramatic victory?

9

"DO YOU WANT TO LOOK at the sweaters?" Nina asked Laura. The sisters were on one of their semiannual trips to Loehmann's in the Bronx. They always went once in the fall and once in the spring.

"Sweaters? It's spring. Why would you want to look at sweaters in the spring?"

"I always look at sweaters. I collect sweaters. Don't you ever wear cotton sweaters in the summer?"

"No," said Laura. "They're too hot. I like loose things in the summer."

"You know how I look in loose things. Like a shopping bag lady."

"Let's look at the pants."

"No way," said Nina. "You can look at the pants. I'll look at you look at the pants. I'm not feeling masochistic enough to try on pants today."

Laura flipped through the pants rack. "Whatever happened with that exterminator you and Ma wanted to use? Did you try him yet?" she asked, as she examined a pair of purple and black striped Lycra bicycle pants.

"Those are great," said Nina, fingering the Lycra.

"Want to try them?"

"I should try them on? Are you kidding? On me they'd make a good pair of fingerless gloves. You try them."

Laura folded them over her arm. "So what happened with the exterminator?"

"I couldn't find out who he was. It was pretty weird. I called that lawyer three times and even wrote him a couple of letters, but I couldn't get anywhere."

"Maybe he was just too lazy to find out for you. Did you offer him a finder's fee?"

"It wasn't just laziness. He was incredibly defensive. Sort of paranoid. It wasn't a pretty scene."

Nina hated playing lawyer for her family. Not that she had to do it very often. On her mother's side was Uncle Irving, who had been playing lawyer for them for fifty years. Ida played social worker and together they had the field covered. On her father's side, enough girl cousins had married real lawyers, with practices of their own, so that they usually didn't have to bother Nina. But every now and then an occasion arose when only Nina would do. And it made her nervous, like she was skirting humiliation. Even though she generally was articulate and had a big enough mouth for the practice of law, she felt she lacked some bulldog instinct necessary for legal greatness. Deep in her heart she knew that some whiny nebbish with two-thirds her IQ could outargue her on any legal point by dint of sheer obstinacy. She couldn't hang in there. The nebbish would just be getting warmed up when Nina would already be at the point of rolling over and playing dead. So every time she had to perform a legal task for a friend or family member, she lived in dread of the discovery of her inef- fectual streak.

With Myron Kaplan she had pushed herself. She had called back three times, threatened suit and subpoenas, and generally made a pain in the ass of herself. It was nauseating, but it was effective lawyering. She would make her mother proud. But she failed.

"Ma is very broken up about this. And there goes my dream of having a cockroach-free apartment by my thirty-fifth birthday."

"That's right, you have a big one coming up. What are you going to do about that?"

"Well, if it's like my last birthday, Grant and I will get Chinese take-out and fight about why he doesn't drink wine."

"I mean what are you going to do about it in a more general sense."

"You mean what am I going to do about my life."

"Do you think you're going to marry Grant?"

"Do you think I'm going to marry Grant?"

"No."

"Why not? Not that I disagree, just out of curiosity."

"I can't explain it, exactly. But I think there's some basic connection missing. If you were both in a room with other people, I'd never pick you two out as a couple. Besides, he's so white-bready."

"Not really white bread. Whole wheat, maybe. Wholesome in a countercultural kind of way. Like he should be living in Ann Arbor. A member of the mung bean culture."

"There's a part of you that's like that."

"Yeah, but the truth is that most of the time it gets on my nerves. I often feel that I'd like to trade him in for someone more decadent. A man who spends his mornings nursing hangovers and smoking Camels."

"You don't have to go overboard. How about something in the middle?"

"You mean like a Jew?"

"You make it sound as if I'm suggesting a leper."

"It's not that I haven't tried, you know. I've known quite a few Jews. In the biblical sense."

"And…?"

And what? Nina had none of the traditional complaints.

Minuscule genitalia, princely demeanor, whining voice—that stuff was all nonsense. It existed in all segments of society. It was none of those things. It was this. There she would be, spending the weekend with Mr. X-berg. Saturday would be fine. They'd go to a lively dinner party and both contribute their share of clever conversation. Followed by acceptably enjoyable sex. Sunday morning she would wake up thinking, It's good to be with a Jew again. We understand each other. It would be a rainy day, so they'd decide to get bagels and sit around with the *Times*. There she'd be, complaining about the vapidity of the "His" column, reading the high-end real-estate classifieds out loud for their dramatic effect, scanning the wedding announcements, and commenting on how many Jews were marrying Jews and how many were marrying WASPs. Mr. X-berg would be getting deeper and deeper into the Sports section. And around noon they would look at each other. And suddenly it would be twenty years ago and she'd be locked up in a Bronx apartment on one of those interminable Sundays with Laura and Ida and Leo. Instead of being the stimulating dinner and bed companion of the previous evening, Mr. X-berg would have grown a head of newsprint, just like her father. And she would know what he was thinking behind the paper—that her previously clever chatter had started to resemble the incessant yakking of his mother, Mrs. X-berg. And to drive the point home, there she would be slicing bagels. They would both jump up and remember how much work they had brought home from the office for the weekend. One of them would flee, and both would sigh with relief.

She tried to simplify the scenario for Laura in twenty-five words or less. "Well, they remind me of Daddy too much. And I remind them of their mothers."

"And it's different with Grant?"

"It's different enough." How was it different? Grant certainly spent enough time hiding behind newsprint, although it wasn't usually the Sports section. But the periods of withdrawal alternated with looks of adoration. And even an occasional flicker of adoration was enough to keep Nina coming back for more.

"Well, if it's mother-father stuff, it sounds like something you could work out in couple therapy."

"Laura, I can't even make it past noon on Sunday with one of those guys. The two of us are never going to make it all the way into the shrink's office."

"Ken and I have worked a lot of this stuff out."

"But you're so different from me."

"In what way?" asked Laura. "We both had Leo Fischman as a father."

How was Laura different? Let her count the ways. "For one thing you talk less." That was the tip of the iceberg, really. Laura had less of a need to be heard. She said what was necessary to keep her life moving along, not to narrate it. She lived life each day without worrying about its story line. "You know how in football there's usually a pair of commentators? One does the play-by-play and the other does the color?"

"I think so."

"Well, I'm the color guy. I have an uncontrollable need to do the color on life. And a lot of these guys just don't appreciate it."

"And Grant appreciates it?"

"He appreciates it more." Because instead of feeling that he was trapped with Mrs. X-berg, yakking into eternity, he was enormously relieved that she was there to remind him that he didn't have to live his life in the icy silence of Wisconsin, where no one ever said anything except 'amen' at the end of each sermon.

"I have four words of advice for you."

"What are they?"

"So shut up already."

Nina laughed. She loved those moments when her sister's Park Slope Jewish matron facade cracked and the voice of Ida Fischman came pouring out. "Because," her sister continued, "Grant is a drip, and I can tell you're not going to marry him."

Nina pondered this. Usually she dismissed whatever her sister said, chalking it up to Laura's incredibly narrow worldview. But when it came to men, Nina was superstitious about what Laura had to say. It always turned out to be right. Her sister was talented in that department.

"It wouldn't hurt if you held your tongue once in a while. Really, Nina, you're the only woman I know who could actually stand to benefit from reading *Cosmopolitan* magazine."

Nina knew her sister's position on passivity was inherently objectionable. Maybe she would try it next time.

"The great thing about marriage," Laura continued, "is that after a point you stop wondering whether you did the right thing and sort of go on automatic pilot. When I got pregnant I became preoccupied with the baby. The millions of men out there ceased to look like possibilities, since they weren't the father of my child."

Nina felt that if she could only skip ahead to the pregnant stage she would be ready to devote herself to the father of her child, whoever he might be. That the millions of men out there would cease to look like possibilities. But she wasn't pregnant and they did seem like possibilities. Millions of possibilities. And none of them working out. It was very overwhelming.

As she looked around Loehmann's, she felt the same way about the endless racks that lined the huge barn of a store. Thank God for Laura, for she was as astute about clothing as she was about men. Nina never went to Loehmann's without her. Besides, the long ride on the IRT to the Bronx was grim if taken unaccompanied. Although it was really no longer than the subway ride from the Upper West Side to Laura's house in Park Slope, which Nina did by herself all the time. It just seemed worse because she was going back to the Bronx, the scene of the crime. There were women who did it alone, the real hard-core shoppers. You'd see them sitting on the IRT, looking very nervous, clutching their Fendi bags for dear life. Size sixes with cellophaned hair, surrounded by welfare mothers with six kids. And at every stop they'd squint to see if they were there yet. Sometimes Nina would have mercy on them and tell them "two more stops" with a friendly wink. Only the stupidest ones asked her how she knew where they were going.

Nina didn't really like to shop anywhere alone. Companions alleviated the anxiety of missed opportunities. Alone, Nina would agonize whenever she came across a great bargain that she couldn't wear. She could never seem to flip through the rack, shrug, say "It's not me," and move on. The fact that something was a great buy was a piece of information that she wanted to do something with. With Laura or a friend there, she could pass the information on. Over the years Nina had cultivated quite a few shopping companions who served a similar purpose. There was the redhead, on whom she could foist all the browns and mustards that Nina couldn't even go near, which broke her heart since she thought them such intelligent colors. And there were several flat-chested friends whom she steered toward all sorts of things with weird cutout tops that made wearing a bra impossible. Then there was the great-legs brigade, including Laura, who patiently tried on an endless parade of leather miniskirts and gave Nina vicarious pleasure. There were tall artistic types with a dramatic demeanor who looked terrific in the purple marabou-trimmed capes that Nina gravitated toward but looked ridiculous in.

Of all her fashion limitations, drama was Nina's greatest disappointment. When she was younger she assumed that her temperament could dictate her fashion requirements. Her hair was either past her waist or a half-inch stubble. Her earrings had to meet a two-inch length requirement. She would try to buy a suit, but the racks of gray flannel would make her skin crawl. She'd inevitably make her way to the P.M. occasion rack and bring home a dress that looked like something Jane Austen would have worn, in some ridiculous shade of chartreuse or magenta. Of course, the P.M. occasions in Nina's life invariably took place in Upper West Side Chinese restaurants. Hardly the place for an eighteenth-century replica ballgown, even in a decent color. It had dawned on Nina slowly that she looked terrible in chartreuse. Gradually she had come to terms with the heartbreaking fact that what she looked best in was rather sedate, after-all-modestly cut clothes in soft colors. With short earrings. Nina felt a great sense of loss. Giving up all those visions of kimonos and satin pants and Hopi earrings. It was like being in a restaurant and knowing you were going to have to order fish for the rest of your life.

Actually that was pretty much true, too. In order not to be fat Nina had to order fish almost all the time. Thoughts of artichoke frittatas and barbecued ribs and custard cakes had to be banished along with chartreuse ballgowns. Neither of these sacrifices seemed impossible, however. She could order fish by telling herself that next time she'd indulge. She was good all week so that she could be bad on the weekend. And she could stick to dove-gray cardigans by dressing her shopping companions in yellow leather pants. But what she couldn't do was get married.

Marriage seemed so ultimate. And you never knew when you were going to run into an incredibly cute artichoke frittata and the thought of having to go home to your fish seemed too much to bear. Marriage wasn't something you could just do during the week. Marriage was deciding that you were going to order fish every single time. And if you ever ordered an arti-choke frittata, you had to do it secretly. And you could never discuss it with anyone afterward. And if you were Catholic, you would have to confess it. And the frittata might make you pregnant or give you a disease and then you'd have to go to the gynecologist and tell him what had happened and swear him to secrecy.

Some people tried to tell her that marriage didn't have to be like that. There could be office flirtations, long lunches, even affairs if she wanted them. Other people tried to make an analogy between marriage and career. You choose a career, they'd say, and when it's no longer right for you, you're free to change it. Marriage is no different, they claimed. But Nina knew this was bullshit. People were always describing their career changes with words like positive and evolving. Divorce in this decade was failure. She voiced this sentiment to her sister.

Laura agreed. "It used to be some sort of coming-of-age ritual for women ten years older than us. But who wants to go through all that pain if you don't have to?"

"What about you?" asked Nina. "Ever kick the idea around?"

"Of course," Laura said without hesitation.

Nina was surprised. "And…?"

"I kick the idea around, but I try not to indulge the impulse too much. Because there's no point. I know I'm not getting divorced, unless something very unusual happens. Like Ken runs off with another woman."

"I wouldn't worry," said Nina. "Ken is a well-socialized Jewish son. Making money is the only socially acceptable channel for his lust. The old saw about them making good husbands still holds. They'll cheat on the IRS, but not on you."

"That's ridiculous. You should see what's going on out there. We were at a dinner party last month, and the guy on my left showed up with his male hairdresser instead of his wife. And this was a Jewish orthodontist, no less. There was another horrible couple there. Actually, now that I think of it, they live in Ma's building. I'd ask her if she knows them, but I can't remember their name.

"What was so horrible about them?"

"He was this very flashy, overbearing guy who snorted with derision at everything his wife said—when he let her say anything, that is. I wish I could remember their name. They live in a duplex, I think."

Nina shook her head. "No way. There are no duplexes in that building. I remember Ma talking about how conservative they are with the alteration permits. And that no one had ever done anything interesting, like a duplex."

"Maybe she doesn't know about it."

"Are you kidding? Our mother, queen of the yentas?"

"Well, this guy said something about a duplex. Maybe he was lying. See what I mean? You can't always trust these guys."

"One thing about Grant. He doesn't lie."

Laura gave Nina a hard look. "One other thing about Grant. You're never going to marry him."

"Enough about men. And enough about pants. They're equally painful topics as far as I'm concerned." She led her sister away from the pants racks. "Let's look at sweaters. They're so much less complicated than either men or pants."

10

IDA WAS EXTREMELY UPSET BY Nina's failure to obtain the name of the exterminator, but she did not take it lying down. "Roach Motels? Never again!" she said thunderously.

"What do you plan on doing about it?" Nina asked her.

Ida thought on her feet. "If we got a sample of the powder, we could have it chemically analyzed and then reproduced."

"You're crazy, Ma. These years of retirement have addled your brain. You better go back to work so you can start thinking straight again."

"What's the big deal? We can have that real estate agent show us Mrs. Gross's apartment again, and while she's not looking we can sneak samples. It'll be fun."

Why couldn't they just shop for wallpaper together, like a normal family? thought Nina. Not the Fischmans. Their idea of a mother-daughter project was stealing cockroach powder samples.

"I don't think we should let anyone know what we're doing," Ida said. "That Myron Kaplan creature was so belligerent that we should avoid unnecessary trouble. Also, I think it's important that we get samples from every room, in case they're using different methods."

Ida was really getting into it. Nina decided to make her happy. "If you really want to do this, I won't stand in your way."

"Another thing. I think you should distract the agent while I take the samples. I'm sure you'll agree that, being the more methodical one, I stand less of a chance of mixing up the samples." Ida had spent decades producing fastidiously neat lesson-plan books. Nina had always proudly cultivated her illegible handwriting. She considered fastidiousness the hobgoblin of a small mind.

"Okay, chief. Whatever you say. You're masterminding this whole adventure."

Patricia White agreed to show them the apartment the following evening.

As Nina walked toward her mother's apartment building, she was struck, as always, with what she referred to as "West End Avenue awe." The street was lined with buildings of similar proportion and facade. It looked like a planned city, an early-twentieth-century version of Brasilia. A pristine strip of middle-class respectability. Of course, these days to buy a little piece of middle-class respectability in Manhattan cost a million dollars.

Nina was crazy about apartment buildings. The way other women dreamed about flower-filled gardens and white picket fences, Nina dreamed about doormen and carpeted hallways. She was soothed and comforted by the great residential fortresses of West End Avenue. She lived on a side street nearby in a walk-up. Forget Scarsdale. You could keep your Tudor-style mansion. All she wanted was an elevator.

To the west, Riverside Drive was an early spring pea green. Nina loved the Drive even more than she loved West End Avenue. It was diverse, almost eccentric, in its architecture. And so romantic and grand that it reminded her of Paris. Nina's romanticization of Manhattan was common in kids who had grown up in the outer boroughs. Of course, children of the suburbs and the rest of America had love affairs with New York, too. But there was something about growing up right next to it, staring at it so closely, that spawned an obsession that never died.

Although Nina had been a neighborhood resident for years, she still found it hard to believe. She couldn't help thinking that without dutiful vigilance she would lose her foothold and wind up back in the Bronx. She saw it happening all the time. Marriage and one kid and there you were, desperately searching for a thousand square feet of space in Riverdale. It was almost a justification of spinster-hood.

Nina turned into her mother's building, a proper specimen of West End Avenue respectability. A green awning, brass plaques, and a blue-uniformed doorman who always made her feel rich. She liked being easily thrilled. Her friends who'd enjoyed more luxury during their childhood were not so easily impressed. Having a low thrill threshold came in handy, like being extremely orgasmic.

Ida let her into the apartment, mouthing "She's here." And there was Patricia White, towering over Ida in her mustard suede heels.

Ida turned to introduce them. "Patricia White, this is my daughter Nina." They shook hands. "We want to thank you so much for showing us the apartment again," Ida continued. "I know how valuable your time is."

"Can I take one more minute of your time while I use the facilities?" Patricia White's voice was timorous.

"Certainly, right down the hall on your right." Ida pointed.

"Yeah," whispered Nina, as they watched Mrs. White slowly progress down the hall, "I can tell her time is real valuable. She had to squeeze us in between a facial and a pedicure. Besides, if her time is so valuable, why does she wear shoes that force her to take ten minutes to walk from room to room?"

"Because she's an idiot. But she does have great legs."

"How many IQ points would you trade for better legs?" Nina asked Ida.

"At this point in my life, none. Now that the rest of my body is gone, what's the point?"

"I figure I could spare ten points for decent legs." If she took all the time she spent trying to find flattering shoes and, worse yet, boots, and spent it improving her mind, she would recoup the points. "The tougher question is whether it's worth a bigger chunk for really great legs. Something that would bring me down to one-twenty."

"One-twenty is still high on the bell curve."

"It's dull normal for the Upper West Side."

Ida picked up her Channel 13 tote bag and showed Nina her specimen containers carefully labeled Bathroom, Kitchen, Living Room, and Bedroom Number One, Two, and Three. The containers were dark blue plastic with snap-on lids. They looked familiar to Nina, but she couldn't quite place them.

"I've seen that deep blue somewhere before," she said. "What are these things?"

"They're for suppositories."

"Of course," said Nina. "How could I forget a thing like that? Suppository blue, one of my favorite colors. Suppose White gets suspicious because you're taking your purse just to go next door. What should we tell her?"

"I don't think suspicion is a major emotion with her. It's canceled out by obliviousness."

"Well, if she asks, tell her you have your tape measure in there."

"I do."

"What for?"

"As a prop."

"Well, maybe you should give it to me. To distract her, I can have her help me measure."

"Okay." Ida handed Nina the tape measure as White tottered back down the hall, clutching her own mustard suede purse tightly.

"Shall we?" White fished the key out of her purse and led them into what was formerly Mrs. Gross's apartment. As Ida scooped powder into her specimen containers, Nina led Patricia White around the apartment, distracting her with a barrage of questions. In the living room, which had a partial river view, she cross-examined White about air rights, lot line windows, and mid-block zoning. It clearly made White nervous, since she seemed to have only a hazy idea of what air rights were.

When Ida gave her the high sign, Nina whisked White off to one of the bathrooms, where she questioned her extensively about the condition of the building's boiler and wiring. White began to squirm. Ida headed off to the bedrooms, and Nina led White into the dining room. She pulled out the tape measure and started measuring. "What shape table would look best here?" she asked, figuring that this was a topic on which Mrs. White would have something to say. She was right.

"Definitely round," said White. "It's the best use of the space. Let's say you're having a dinner party for eight, which I think is the ideal number for a dinner party, don't you?"

"Yes, ideal, assuming you can find seven other people you can stand." Women like White always brought out the Bronx in Nina. They made her assume a demeanor some-what like a hostile Catskills comedian. But White seemed not to hear.

"Some people prefer six," she continued, "but then you run the risk of having the other two couples not hit it off. Which makes you play go-between all night. With eight, you can relax and let them entertain themselves. Of course, it's more work in the kitchen, but only just a bit. Eight is quite manageable, I've always found. Even without having anyone in."

"Having anyone in what?"

"Having anyone in. You know, to help." White threw her a sharp look, but quickly slipped into her remembrance of dinner parties past. "And with a round table, no one is too far away from the centerpiece. I used to have a lovely round table in my breakfast room, which I used for luncheons and brunches. I had a square silver bowl that I would fill with roses. I liked the contrast between the square bowl and the round table. My goodness, I haven't thought about that bowl in ages. I gave it to my eldest daughter when she got married. Let's see, what did we say this room measured?"

"It's about twelve feet square. Not exactly palatial dimensions."

"But that's the beauty of a round table, you see. A forty-eight-inch round seats six to eight quite comfortably, believe me. And you need two and a half feet of chair clearance on either side. Now, forty-eight inches is how many feet?"

Nina waited for White to answer her own question. When she realized the agent had no intention of doing the calculation, Nina answered. "Four feet."

"Okay. And two and half on either side adds another what?"

"Five."

"Which gives us…?"

"Nine." Was this woman testing her or was she brain-damaged? How could someone who was brilliant enough to wear mustard pumps with a teal suit be too dumb to add four and five?

"And we've got twelve feet in this room, right? So there you go. With a round table, you can have lovely dinner parties for eight."

"Well, actually it's my sister and her husband who are thinking about buying this apartment. I don't think she has a round table."

"That's too bad. It's one thing to buy a new table. But it can be heartbreaking to have to change all your tablecloths. You can get very attached to tablecloths."

"I got attached to a napkin once. That was heartbreaking, too, in its own way."

Mrs. White knew enough to change the subject. "Where in the world is your mother?"

"Since she had seen the apartment before, she made a list of specific details she wanted to check out this time."

"Such as…?"

Nina thought fast. "She wanted to see if my sister's paella pan would fit in the oven." It sounded ridiculous, but it might just be the kind of thing that White could relate to.

"But of course she'll have the kitchen redone, won't she? Those appliances are unusable." There was a break in the obliviousness, and suspicion was starting to shine through. "Shall we join your mother?"

"Hurry up, Ma," Nina shouted in warning. "I'm already late."

Ida reappeared. "I'm ready."

"Did you get a feeling for the place?" White asked.

"Yeah, Ma, did you get the scoop?"

"Got the scoop," said Ida.

"Okay, let's blow this pop stand," said Nina. "And thank you again for your time, Mrs. White. I know how valuable it is."

"My pleasure," said White, as she tottered off toward the door.

ααα

"Now what the hell are we going to do with these?" said Nina, once they were back in Ida's apartment.

"Have them chemically analyzed." Ida proudly lined up the suppository containers on the dining room table.

"What does that mean, exactly? Do we look in the Yellow Pages under Chemical Analysis?"

Ida shrugged. "I have absolutely no idea."

"Let's give them to Ken. Maybe he'll know how to get

them chemically analyzed." Nina was trying to learn how to delegate. It was tough, since she wasn't a natural delegator. It was a terrible problem in the office, where work would pile up on her desk and never leave. She felt like a fish swimming in a tank choked with algae. Not that there was anyone around the office you could really delegate anything to. Understaffed was a concept that permeated the place. But some of the other lawyers seemed to be more clever at delegating. So it was up there on Nina's list of things to do: throw out rotten vegetables, do leg lifts, learn to delegate. She tried to practice whenever she got the chance.

"Ken must know someone at a lab," Nina continued. "Like when he scrapes things off people's bodies. Doesn't he say 'I'll have to send this to the lab'? Why can't he just send over the cockroach powder instead of someone's mole?"

"I suppose he could," Ida said with a sigh, "if he didn't think the whole thing was too ridiculous."

"Well, we won't ask him," said Nina, practicing her delegating skills. "We'll just give him the specimens and tell him to do it. That always works better. Now, when should we do this? Are you planning to see them soon?"

"I'm supposed to go out to the beach for Mother's Day weekend." The Rubins had a house in the Hamptons. It was on the bay side, not the ocean side, but it still intimidated both Ida and Nina. "Why don't you come out with me?"

"You know I hate spending the weekend out there. I find it enervating."

"We could take the train out together on Saturday night. That way I won't have to sell my Saturday afternoon ballet ticket. I'd prefer it to driving out with Ken and Laura, actually. I hate sitting in the back between the kids' car seats. It makes me a little nauseated."

"The house makes me nauseated."

"The house makes you jealous," said Ida. "Admit it."

"The house makes me nauseated with jealousy. But I think going out with you is a good idea. Ken's always more responsive when he's out at the beach. Between the two of us, I'm sure we can talk him into sending these samples to the lab."

Nina smiled. She was starting to enjoy this. It was proving more interesting than shopping for wallpaper after all. Too bad she had to wait until Mother's Day.

11

NINA STOOD IN THE HALLWAY of housing court, reading that day's calendar. The hallway was where all the action took place. It was jam-packed with landlords, tenants, and attorneys. Nina had six cases on that day. Two were in Part A, three were in Part C, and one was in Part D. Which meant she had to scurry between the three different court-rooms, checking to see if a case had been called. It wasn't as nerve-racking as it sounded, though. She'd been hanging around housing court long enough so that the court officers knew her and wouldn't default her if she didn't appear exactly on time. But it was hectic, very hectic.

It was especially hectic today, since one of her clients didn't speak English. Nina's Spanish was decent but not fluent. She did, however, have an extensive working vocabulary of all the landlord-tenant words. Heat, rent, dispossess. The way all the words she knew in Yiddish related to food.

She could speak Spanish because all the children of the left could speak Spanish. At the end of sixth grade they asked you if you wanted to take Spanish or French. For kids like her it wasn't really a choice. Even though you were only eleven, you knew you had to take Spanish so that one day you could work in the community. At an age when most kids didn't have the word community in their vocabulary, the red-diaper babies could write you an essay.

And here was Nina, almost thirty-five and still working in the community. It felt like an arranged marriage. She had made her peace with it. But love and passion? No, there was neither. Not like with Grant and his work. He had turned his back on his traditional roots and consciously sought out poverty law. And after all these years he still retained a fierce passion for it. It was like an intermarriage where the husband and wife fought against all odds and love conquered all. Adversity only served to cement the bond.

Law would never make her heart pound or her spirit soar. Nina had known that from the first day of law school when her attention wandered off during a contracts class and had yet to return. But despite her ambivalence, she knew now that law school hadn't been a mistake. For one thing, being a lawyer looked good on her resume. It was like wearing a button that said "I have a high IQ." Before she became a lawyer she had been a secretary. She really could have used such a button then. Being a secretary was like being permanently stuck in junior high school. No one paid any attention to anything you said. Actually, housing court was a lot like junior high school, too. Everyone screamed and interrupted you all the time. But unlike junior high school, if things got really bad you could get people's attention by saying "Your Honor, may I approach the bench?" Also you could go to the bathroom without a hall pass.

Out in the hallway, Nina went over Mrs. Rodriguez's defense on her non-payment case. Mrs. Rodriguez stood anxiously by. She was having a problem with the Social Security Administration and as a result was a few months behind on her rent. Nina made a list. No heat for three weeks in February. A chunk of plaster had fallen from the bedroom ceiling. What would Nina do without the warranty of habitability? She'd be out of a job.

"Que mils?" asked Nina.

"Cucarachas, " said Mrs. Rodriguez.

It was only good using cockroaches when there was an infant in the house. That way when the judge yelled "Everyone has cockroaches in New York—even I have cockroaches," you could describe how they crawled around in the baby's crib.

"Hay bebes en su casa?"

"No."

Well, that wouldn't work. "Hay ratas?" asked Nina. Rats were still worth something in housing court. Mrs. Rodriguez shook her head. She didn't have rats. Well, Nina would see what she could do. She could at least buy a couple of weeks while Mrs. Rodriguez straightened out what had happened to her Social Security check.

Nina's mind wandered back to cockroaches. She smiled and thought about Ida stealing powder samples from Mrs. Gross's apartment. It seemed wild, but they had always planned little adventures for themselves, ever since Nina was a kid. Ida and the girls would get on buses and go to visit other cities. Leo would stay home and read I. F. Stone's Weekly. He never seemed to need those little adventures. He'd had enough adventures in the Communist party and the Second World War. So in Nina's mind, travel and adventure were woman's domain. Men were something you stayed home with. When other women balked at going somewhere unaccompanied, Nina never knew what they were talking about. Did they expect their mothers to go everywhere with them?

Grant fit this pattern perfectly. He was either working or at home reading. He had a list of subscriptions to leftist periodicals that rivaled her father's. Maybe they should move in together. She could have him installed, like a fixture. Then when she came home from the ballet, there he would be, plugged in and lit up. It was good to keep a light on at night. It kept the burglars away and the cockroaches in hiding. But having Grant move in would mean living with ten years' worth of back issues of the *Nation*. And it would certainly curtail her adventures. Because sometimes her adventures required an overnight stay.

There was one of her adventures in the hallway right now. Mike Nitkin. He had shaved his beard, but he still looked good to her. She had been his last fling before he married a pediatrician. They always married the next one. Nina had a career as a romantic penultimate.

"Hi, Mike. How are you?" He had a baby now, so she prepared herself for five minutes on chicken pox, which had been going around lately. But he had a surprise for her.

"Guess what? I'm leaving the office and going to work for a firm."

She was shocked. Mike Nitkin had the poverty lawyer syndrome bad. He had a closetful of corduroy suits and had been wearing the same wire-frame glasses since 1969. How would he survive on the outside?

"How exciting. You must be a nervous wreck. I mean, after all these years."

"No, actually, I'm looking forward to it." He seemed determinedly calm. "I'll see you later, Nina. I've got a motion to argue." Mike squeezed her elbow and ran down the hall.

If he could do it, maybe she should. Instead of obsessing about whether or not to leave Grant, maybe she should obsess about whether or not to leave her job. She couldn't leave both at the same time, since each would probably result in a twenty-pound weight gain. If she left both simultaneously, she'd gain forty and have to shop at Lane Bryant. And there was no way she could put herself through searching for a job and looking for a man at the same time. Well, let's see, which was less of a glut on the market, being a lawyer or being an unattached woman? They were both oversubscribed fields.

She was amazed how hard change had become for her these days. In the past she had prided herself on playing out her life before an ever-changing backdrop. Seven different majors in college. Twenty-eight different roommates, if you counted up the transient hordes that drifted into and out of the five bedrooms of her drafty old off-campus house. Backpacking around Europe, she had squeezed twelve different countries into a summer. And almost as many men.

Nothing much had changed for the past five years, though. Grant, her job, her apartment. She was finally rent-stabilized in every sense of the word. It was comforting in a way. If she were still carrying on the way she did when she was younger, she'd have mononucleosis for sure. Or Epstein-Barr virus, that new thing that was going around striking people who tried too hard. So what if change was something she only did when she went from the express to the local? She could live with that. Most of the time.

"Miss Fischman?" Mort Horowitz's head was poking out of Part B. Mort was a creature indigenous to housing court. He was a partner in the firm of Horowitz & Horowitz, an eviction mill. But he was definitely the second Horowitz. His brother Milt brought in the business, kept the office running, and sent Mort down to shuffle around the halls of justice on a daily basis. She had met Milt once, when he made a rare court appearance. Their associate had been stranded out of town and Mort was hospitalized with colitis. Milt and Mort looked almost identical, except that Milt's suit was composed of natural fibers. They both wore toupees.

Nina checked her file. Horowitz & Horowitz would be handling the Rodriguez matter. Her paralegal had scrawled a memo to the file. It said that the Social Security problem would probably resolve itself. Another three weeks would be helpful.

"Mr. Horowitz," Nina called down the hall, "I'm ready for trial." It was the usual first line in her adjournment scenario.

"Can't we settle this thing?" Mort shuffled toward her.

"I'm ready for trial," she repeated firmly.

Mort looked at her mournfully. Most of the old guys looked at her that way, as if she were their own child who had betrayed them. The younger guys usually flashed her looks of pure hatred. At times like this, she tried picturing her sister in her place, provoking looks of mourning or hatred all day instead of chats with pleasant shopkeepers and other young moms. It was a stretch.

"My client isn't here," Mort whined.

"That's your problem, isn't it?" Nina said crisply. "I'm going to have the case marked off the calendar."

"Okay, okay," said Mort, dutifully playing his role. "How much time do you want?"

"I need six weeks. My client has to go to the Dominican Republic. She has a sick child there whom she has to visit." Sometimes it seemed like all she did was buy time for her clients. They should offer Adjournments 101 in law school.

"Six weeks! I can't give you six weeks. She hasn't paid her rent in four months. My client is being bled dry. Tell her to come back in two weeks."

"I told you, she has to go to the Dominican Republic. She can't make it back in two weeks. A month would be acceptable."

"All right, three weeks. Is that what you want?"

"That would be all right. Let's put it down for May twenty-fourth."

"That's more than three weeks. Oh, all right already. The twenty-fourth. You'll tell the clerk?" Nina nodded and Mort shuffled on to his next appearance.

On her way back to Part B, Nina stopped to recheck her

cases on the court calendar posted in the hallway. The list included all the cases on for that day—1345 Corp. v. Johnson, Weinstein v. Ramos. The usual grist for the landlord-tenant mill. Halfway down the list she spotted something very interesting: West Estates, N. V., v. Singer.

The urge was irresistible. "West Estates. Anyone here from West Estates?" she yelled up and down the hallway. It was the customary method of locating your adversary in housing court.

A young blond man in an expensive suit carrying a monogrammed briefcase almost made it to the door. At the last minute he turned and approached Nina. She recognized the look of smug distaste. Clearly he was the H. Pennington Wells creature who had tried to evict Steve's old-lady client, Mrs. Kahn.

"What do you want?" he asked Nina. "The case has been adjourned."

What did she want? She didn't really know, but couldn't pass up the opportunity for a fishing expedition. Holding this guy's attention would be difficult. She had never seen anyone want to get the hell out of someplace so bad. Nina summoned up a kittenish demeanor. It didn't come naturally to her. She remembered her sister's remark at Loehmann's. Maybe she should give *Cosmopolitan* a look. "You've just got to satisfy my curiosity about something," she said, attempting to purr. Unfortunately it came out more like a growl.

"What's that?" he snapped.

"I didn't know that West Estates owned any buildings in Manhattan. What neighborhood is this one in?" It was lame, but it was a start.

"Apartment," H. Pennington Wells grunted.

"Excuse me?" She couldn't bring herself to flutter her eyelashes, but she did manage to stick her tits out a little farther.

"They own the apartment, not the building, It's a co-op on West End Avenue."

"And what's this eviction proceeding all about?"

"Primary residence. The tenant moved to Florida, but she won't give up the apartment."

Under New York City rent laws, that wasn't kosher.

"So I assume she's elderly?" Nina flung her hair about a bit. "I mean if she's moved to Florida she must be. Why would anyone else move there, right?"

Another little old lady on West End Avenue. Kahn, Gross, and now Singer. Highly unusual, Nina thought. But what did it mean?

H. Pennington Wells looked at Nina, then at his watch, and turned toward the door. "I have no idea. And I'm late." She put her hand on his elbow, but he opened the door. "I have to go."

Nina gave up. If her hair and her tits didn't do it, she didn't have much else to work with.

"Can I have your card?" she called after him, making one last attempt.

This time he didn't even stop. "No," he called over his shoulder and was gone.

Before she left court that day, she made sure to write down the index number of West Estates, N. V., v. Singer.

12

"**I**T STINKS." Nina sniffed as she and Ida settled themselves into a Long Island Rail Road car.

"But it's a non-smoker," Ida said. "They all are now."

"It clearly had a long history as a smoking car," said Nina. "I'm sure they'll stink for the next twenty years."

"Are you going to complain all the way out to Westhampton? It's not so bad. At least we miss all the traffic."

"I don't know. When I was younger, I was obsessive about never spending a summer weekend in the city. More and more I find myself thinking the hell with it. I'd be just as happy to stay home, see the new Debra Winger movie at the Loews Eighty-fourth Street, and save myself the aggravation."

"I do like Debra Winger." Ida nodded. "You look a little like her."

"That's what every Jewish mother tells her daughter." Twenty years ago it was Streisand. It was as if Hollywood had a quota of one for women without nose jobs and they only let one onto the screen every two decades. "Anyway," Nina continued, "not everyone feels the way I do. There are people who are single and have thin thighs who'll go out to the Hamptons no matter what."

"And the ones without thin thighs?"

"Go to the Berkshires, where they can sit on the lawn at Tanglewood with a long skirt gracefully arranged around their legs and flirt with dignity."

"What about Fire Island?" asked Ida. "Is that the same as the Hamptons?"

Nina thought back to her summers on Fire Island. People were different in the Hamptons and on Fire Island. In the Hamptons, people jumped into their cars and drove around to tennis courts, movie theaters, restaurants, and discotheques. They had organized party networks for both social and professional purposes. On Fire Island there were no cars and nothing to do. Everyone just sort of listlessly hung out. Real achiever types went crazy on Fire Island. On a rainy Saturday in the Hamptons, it wouldn't be unusual for someone to spend the morning scouring the East End for esoteric cooking ingredients or comparison-shopping for strawberries and then devote the entire afternoon to testing some complicated recipe. On Fire Island, if it looked like rain on Saturday, they'd just pull out a jug of cheap wine and a box of Wheat Thins and curl up with back issues of *New York* magazine.

"Fire Island's a little raunchier," she said. "There are more underachievers there. I, of course, prefer it." The Hamptons made her nervous. All those people in tennis whites. Ken played a lot of tennis. She pictured him in his Topsiders waiting at the station with the Range Rover while she and her mother lumbered off the train, their ethnic earrings swinging, like visitors from the old country.

"Do you have the samples?" Nina asked her mother.

"They're right here." Ida pointed to her omnipresent Channel 13 tote bag.

"Let's wait until after dinner to ask him. He always feels

expansive after he's barbecued. Like he's successfully completed brain surgery."

"Too bad he doesn't drink," Ida said.

"He drinks wine."

"Doesn't count." Ida had spent most of her life drinking whiskey sours and Cherry Heering. Lately Nina had noticed her mother ordering vodka and tonic and even throwing back a few scotches. Nina viewed her mother's new habit with pride. She was a scotch man herself.

Later that evening, after Ken had skillfully grilled salmon steaks, and Nina and Ida had nodded with appreciation each time he pointed out the fresh dill, Ida pulled the specimens out of her tote bag. Nina explained what they wanted.

"A couple of nut jobs, that's what you two are," he said. He pretended to be outraged, but he was obviously getting a huge kick out of the whole thing. "Everyone else has a mother-in-law who brings him chicken soup in a jar. I have one who brings me cockroach powder in a suppository container. How did I ever marry into such a family?"

Nina often asked herself a similar question, which was how did Ken and Laura stay married to each other? Of course, they were the perfect couple in most people's minds. But they were so different from each other. Did that tend to make them a perfect couple or a ridiculous couple? Nina couldn't tell. When she evaluated men for their relationship potential, she looked for someone who reminded her of herself. Her friends knew that the most promising thing she could report after a first date was "He's just like me." Nina remembered all of the just-like-me's who didn't pan out. "He's just like me— he prefers grapefruit juice to orange." "He's just like me—he liked *Bananas* better than *Sleeper*." "He's just like me—a Gemini with a Sagittarius ascendant." The fact that they had a wife in Cleveland or were facing indictment for white-collar crimes seemed secondary. Of course, Grant wasn't just like her, but at first she had been convinced that he was. What was it she had said? Something like "He's just like me—he'd rather try a case in front of Judge Montana than Judge Powers."

Nina also often applied the that's-something-I-would-say test, which Ken and Laura flunked miserably. If you handed Nina a slip of paper with a quote on it, she would know instantly whether Laura or Ken had said it. There was no overlapping, no gray area. Their minds were separate and distinct. If you were to draw a Venn diagram of them, there would be no crosshatched area. Did they balance each other nicely? Were they two halves of a very healthy whole? Or were they both clinging to antiquated sex roles, creating a diseased and reactionary existence? It was a close call. For no matter how antiquated and reactionary it seemed, it obviously worked well. The machinery was well oiled. When Laura referred all questions of substance to Ken, she did it without resentment and he accepted without contempt. They seemed affectionate and companionable.

Nina would remind herself how unstimulating Laura's life must be, home all day with the kids with only a few hours a week of furniture stripping to give it meaning. But Laura seemed happier than anyone Nina knew. Certainly happier than Nina, driving herself crazy all the time with Should I be a lawyer, Should I marry Grant, Should I this, Should I that. And happier than Nina's friends who had children and careers. Working their butts off, they claimed, for ten grand a year after child-care costs. And dealing with the guilt, exhaustion, and money worries.

Ken seemed as content as Laura. He enjoyed his role in the family and never gave any indication that he found his wife narrow or boring. There seemed no need to worry about his straying. Except for an almost imperceptible flicker of arousal that Nina knew she could evoke in him. It happened at times like this. "A couple of nut jobs," he had said after Nina explained the chemical analysis she and Ida wanted done. He said it with fondness and a sense of enjoyment. But there was something else behind it that Nina knew she wasn't imagining. He was sexually aroused.

It was a syndrome she often detected in husbands. The way other women could fill them with wistful longing simply by crossing their legs or straightening their sweaters. Nina could do it with a one-liner. She could see it in their eyes. Instead of fantasizing about all the leggy blondes with great tits they'd never had and never would have, they would think about all the clever comments and interesting insights they were missing. But the effect was the same. It made their cocks hard. Nina had once read about this syndrome in a Woody Allen story called "The Whore of Mensa."

Nina knew it was just the novelty that was stimulating to them. If she were married to these guys, forcing them to share her insights night after night, they'd get sick of it. The way that husbands of Playboy bunnies started taking their wives' great tits for granted. But it was still a kick when it happened. So when Ken sat there saying "a couple of nut jobs" and getting stiff, it made Nina go at it even harder. She liked knowing that, ever so slightly, under the authentic reproduction Shaker table and the Laura Ashley tablecloth, his cock was swelling.

"At least we have good skin," Nina said. "We don't bother you with rashes or make you pop our pimples. There's a woman in my office whose brother-in-law is a gynecologist and he does her Pap smears every year. Pretty weird, huh?"

"Pap smear," yelled Danielle from the other end of the table where she had been quietly making ice cream soup. "I want a Pap smear on a bagel."

"That's schmear, not smear. A schmear on a bagel," said Ken.

"Then give me a Pap schmear on a bagel," Danielle insisted.

"When you're older, you can have all the Pap schmears you want, dear. You're too young now."

"Mommy, why are Grandma and Aunt Nina giving Daddy baby powder? Is it for Jared?"

"It's not baby powder, it's cockroach powder. To get rid of roaches," Laura explained.

"But why did they bring it to this house? We don't have our cockroaches here. We keep them in our other house, in Brooklyn."

So the secret was out. The Rubin cockroach collection was finally revealed.

"It's not for our cockroaches. Daddy's going to take it to work and see what it's made of. It's like when we make cookies. We put in flour and butter and sugar. Well, somebody put a bunch of different things together to make this cockroach powder and we want to see what they used."

Danielle picked up an open container and inspected it. "It looks like flour and sugar," she said. "But no eggs and no chocolate chips."

Pap schmear on a bagel. That was pretty good. The kid had an interesting mind, thought Nina approvingly. Then she stopped herself. So what? Why monitor a four-year-old for interesting thoughts? What if she didn't have an interesting mind? What if she wasn't funny? What if she wasn't unusual? What if she never did anything that hadn't already been featured on the cover of *Time* in an article about her generation? What would happen to her? Maybe she'd be doomed to spend her weekends in her house in the Hamptons surrounded by her two lovely children and her Shaker furniture. Maybe she'd have to spend her mornings clipping lilies and peonies from her garden and her afternoons arranging them in crystal vases. Maybe she'd have to spend her summers going strawberry picking and putting up preserves and her autumns going apple picking and baking pies. Instead of getting her letters printed in the *Times* and knowing every neighborhood in New York well enough to drive a cab. Big deal. So what if Danielle's mind didn't turn out interesting enough to give somebody else's husband an erection under the table? So what if she had to rely on her great tits or her wedding ring? She could survive. Sometimes it seemed to Nina that an interesting mind and a token could get you on the subway.

"So it's settled," said Nina. "You're going to get the stuff analyzed, right?"

"This is ridiculous." Ken shook his head.

"C'mon," said Ida. "It can be your Mother's Day present to me."

"I guess I know some guy who could break it down for me."

"Awright!" whooped Nina. "Danielle, gimme a high five."

Danielle ran over and slapped palms with her aunt. This child was well trained. Nina was always trying to teach her niece schoolyard survival skills. It was like giving her anti-ballet lessons. It was probably pointless. Danielle didn't look like the kind of kid who would be spending much time in a schoolyard. At four, she already favored Liberty of London prints.

Danielle's wardrobe was almost as beautiful as the Hamptons house, which was quite beautiful indeed. The living room featured white canvas duck couches and a few pine pieces. An airier feeling than the overstuffed chintz in the city, but no less elegant. There were Shaker reproductions in the dining room, complete with a peg rack on which to hang the chairs when you wanted to sweep. Nina rarely had the urge to sweep, but if she had someplace to hang her chairs, she might be more inclined to do so. And she had to admit that Ken was okay as far as husbands went. He dominated benevolently. The whole setup was pretty seductive. Almost enough to make you want to sell yourself into the Jewish slave trade.

13

NINA'S ANSWERING MACHINE showed four messages. All of them were from her mother. The first one said that Ida had gotten a message from Ken that said he had the results of the chemical analysis. The second one said that Ida called Ken back and didn't get him. The third one said that Ken called Ida back and didn't get her. The fourth one said that she called Ken back and he said that they had found digitalis in one of the samples. Ida believed in liberal phone use. When it came to reaching out and touching someone, she was a regular octopus.

Nina picked up the phone, put it down again, and pulled off her pantyhose. She was dying to find out more, but pantyhose removal was always first priority with her. Not that she wasn't grateful for their invention. She firmly believed that if women were still forced to wear girdles and stockings, none of them would ever want to get dressed and go to work. They would still be wandering around all day in housedresses and slippers, like the women in the Bronx of her childhood.

After she removed her pantyhose, she inspected their toes. The toe runs on one side had gone too far past the shoe line for acceptability. Nina was not one of those fastidious types who cut off one leg, found a matching amputee, and salvaged them. She was one of those less fastidious types who was too lazy to even cross the room to put the pantyhose in the garbage. She tossed them in the general direction of the wastepaper basket and let them lie where they fell as she turned to dial her mother.

Ida answered immediately. "Did you get my message?"

"Yeah. Isn't digitalis a medicine?"

"And a poison. Don't you read Agatha Christie?" Ida said impatiently. "They're always brewing it from foxglove leaves."

Nina used to read Agatha Christie novels in college. They were a good accompaniment to marijuana. These days she could barely make her way through Section C of the *Times*, much less pick up a book. That still put her ahead of her sister, whose reading material seemed to consist solely of the White Flower Farms garden catalog.

"I'm coming right over," said Ida. "And don't fall asleep before I get there." During the Agatha Christie marijuana era, Nina used to stay up until three. Now she struggled to stay up past nine-thirty.

"I won't fall asleep. But I want to warn you, Grant's coming over in about fifteen minutes."

"Good. I'd be interested to hear what he has to say about this." Ida wasn't a big Grant fan—she could never relate on an emotionally intimate level with someone who was a full foot taller than she was—but she respected his way of thinking. Politically Ida and Grant had achieved a meeting of minds. They had both forged their beliefs in a climate where it was possible to hope for true social and racial equality and harmony. The idealisms of post-McCarthy Wisconsin and that of the Hunter College class of 1938 bore a remarkable similarity to each other. Nina had forged her beliefs in a climate where everyone was busy trying not to get beaten up in the junior high school bathroom, and with Leo Fischman scream-ing "dirty Nazi bastards" from be-hind the evening newspaper. It was less conducive to idealism.

Nina made a few feeble attempts to straighten up her apartment before Grant and Ida arrived. She picked up her pantyhose and threw them away. She washed the cups and glasses that were piled up in her sink. That was all that she ever had to wash, actually. Everything she ate came in a dis-posable container. She straightened the kitchen a bit. It was-n't so much a kitchen as a refrigerator, sink, and stove lining the wall on one side of the living room, separated from the rest of the room by her bureau. On top of her bureau she had placed a butcher block, which served as kitchen counter space. Nina did have a bedroom, but it was too small to hold both a bed and a bureau.

She had an old coffee table of her mother's, piled high with mail and magazines. Nina cleaned it off, threw the piles into the bedroom, and put out a bowl of oranges. She kept oranges around because they rotted more slowly than other fruits. And no one actually ever went to the trouble of peeling and eating one, so even if they were a bit over the hill, it was hard to tell. They were more like props than food.

The intercom buzzed. Nina buzzed back. The listen but-ton had long ago stopped working, so it was always a leap of faith to let someone in. Nina's apartment was a fourth-floor walk-up. This was extremely convenient for her, since she was able to get a great deal of her apartment cleaned between the lobby buzzer and the doorbell. Nina always worked well under a deadline. This evening she made her bed, threw her laundry into the closet, and wiped the toothpaste ring off the sink while either Grant or Ida trudged up the four flights. Judging by the amount of time it was taking, she bet it was Ida. It turned out, however, that Ida and Grant had arrived together.

Nina was a little embarrassed. She and Grant were well

past the point where he expected champagne and a negligée when he came over. But he didn't quite expect her mother.

"Mom's here on an emergency basis," Nina began to explain.

"I know," he said. "She told me a little about it on the way up. Now tell me the whole story."

"Nina hasn't mentioned any of this to you before?" asked Ida.

"Nothing."

"He's not as interested in exterminating as we are."

"Well, in a nutshell, this is what's happened to date," Ida said. "I've had a cockroach problem that I've been battling for years. My neighbor Mrs. Gross, on the other hand, never seemed to have any roaches. After she died, my son-in-law wanted to take a look at her apartment. He thought he might want to buy and resell it."

"Did Mrs. Gross own it?" asked Grant.

"No, she was a non-purchasing tenant. A few years after the building converted, the original landlord sold her apartment to a Netherlands Antilles corporation. Anyway, I went with my son-in-law and a real-estate agent to look at the apartment and noticed that there was absolutely no evidence of roaches. There was also a white powder spread around the place that was clearly a method of exterminating. That reminded me of the fact that this Netherlands Antilles corporation had always sent a special exterminator to Mrs. Gross's apartment. They never used the regular building exterminator."

"How did you know that?" asked Grant.

"As a member of the board of directors, I am in close contact with the managing agent who had mentioned it to me over the years. Also, I had discussed the matter with Mrs. Gross. We were friendly."

"My mother's an incurable yenta. That's the kind of thing she would know."

"Do you know what a yenta is, Grant?" Ida asked kindly.

"Of course he knows what a yenta is, Ma. He's lived in New York for a decade. Don't get him started on showing off his Yiddish. He'll never stop."

"Anyway," Ida continued, "after I saw Mrs. Gross's empty apartment, I was very impressed with how roach-free it was. I decided to call that exterminator to see if he would do my apartment also. But the lawyer who is the contact person for the owner of the apartment refused to give me the name. He was surprisingly hostile and defensive to my innocent request. So Nina and I went back to the apartment with the real estate agent and stole samples of the white powder. We stole one sample from each room and made a notation as to which room it came from. Just in case they were using different compounds in different rooms. Then we gave the samples to my son-in-law to have chemically analyzed. He called today to tell me that the samples taken from the kitchen contained digitalis in a fairly high quantity."

"It wasn't in any of the other samples?" asked Nina.

"No, only the kitchen sample. Now, digitalis is a medication that people with a heart condition take. But it is also a deadly poison that can be used to simulate a heart attack. I know this from reading mystery novels. And my son-in-law tells me that this is indeed true."

"So the digitalis kills roaches by giving them a heart attack?" asked Grant.

Nina was glad he was there to ask the stupid questions.

"I think you're missing the point," said Ida. "The digitalis was only in the kitchen sample. The rest of the matter was a silicon compound that kills roaches by asphyxiating them. Apparently they walk through the powder, lick their little feet, and after the stuff gets into their system it chokes them to death."

"So why was there digitalis in the kitchen?" asked Grant.

"It clearly wasn't there to kill roaches," said Ida. "The silicon compound was also there. So in terms of roach-killing, the presence of the digitalis was superfluous."

"What was it doing there?" he asked again.

Ida paused dramatically. "Clearly Mrs. Gross was meant to eat it. I'm sure she was poisoned."

"That's crazy," said Grant. "How could she have been poisoned by cockroach powder? Was she in the habit of eating it?"

"It could have gotten on her dishes or something," Nina suggested. She liked this poison theory. It had great plot potential.

"That's ridiculous," said Grant. "She wouldn't have eaten off of a dish with powder all over it."

"It's a powerful substance," said Ida. "Even an imperceptible amount would have been lethal. I don't know how she ingested it. But I'm convinced we have a murder on our hands."

"It's possible." Grant nodded thoughtfully. "But you have one problem."

"What's that?"

"Intent," said Grant. "You'll never get a murder conviction. Let's assume that the digitalis somehow made it into Mrs. Gross's body and poisoned her. In terms of prosecuting a crime, you'll never be able to prove the intent that you need for murder."

"Why not?" Nina was beginning to pout. She felt like a child who had just had a toy taken away.

"The whole thing has to have been an accident. No one poisons anyone by hoping they'll get cockroach powder on their dishes and end up eating it. Now if you're looking to prove criminal negligence as opposed to murder, you'd have an easier time. There you don't need to prove intent. And you can get a conviction against the landlord."

"It might be easier to prove than murder," said Nina, "but

what's the point? It doesn't answer any of the interesting questions, like what was the digitalis actually doing there? Who put it there and why?"

"But the beauty of a criminal negligence case is that it doesn't matter how the digitalis got there. It was mixed in with the cockroach powder that was distributed by the exterminator, who was an agent of the landlord. And a reasonable landlord either knew or should have known that the powder contained a lethal substance. Therefore, it was criminally negligent for him not to take precautions to ensure that the cockroach powder was safe for use as an exterminating agent."

"That's the problem with law," Nina whined. "You have a juicy little murder and it gets reduced to elements of proof and you end up with a conviction that has no meaning."

"What do you do in a case like this?" asked Ida, being less theoretical and more practical. "Do you just walk into the police station?"

"I'll tell you what will happen if you walk into the police with this evidence. They'll laugh. They'll tell you that the old lady's heart medicine probably fell out of her bottle and somehow got crushed into the roach powder."

"But she didn't take heart medicine," said Ida. "I would have known if she was on heart medication. Her heart was in terrific shape."

"I'm telling you, they're not going to pay attention to you. If you really want this thing investigated, you have to handle it in a politically shrewd manner."

"I don't understand," said Ida.

Grant turned to Nina. "Remember that lead-based paint case I was working on a couple of years ago?"

"Vaguely." When it came to Grant's cases she was always vague.

"You remember. It was that landlord in East Harlem who

was still using lead-based paint after all these years. And he knew there were babies in the building who were eating the paint chips and getting poisoned. So we went to the district attorney's office and got them to prosecute the landlord for criminal negligence."

"What happened?" asked Ida.

"We settled the case. The landlord stripped and repainted the entire building and made some kind of restitution. But it was easy to get the D.A.'s office interested. They love to prosecute landlords these days because it makes such good headlines."

"So you're saying that if we can get the D.A. interested by offering him some good pro-tenant press, we might end up getting this murder solved," said Nina.

"This alleged murder," said Grant. "Why don't I call the assistant district attorney who worked on the lead-based paint case with me? I think he still works there. Maybe he'll see you. His name is Judah Lev."

14

JUDAH LEV WAS A LITTLE TWERP. Make that a smug little twerp, thought Nina. On the wall behind his desk hung his diplomas, one of them in Hebrew. They were all laminated. Nina hated laminated diplomas. They reminded her of plastic slipcovered furniture. The center one was from the University of Michigan Law School, dated five years ago. That would make this guy around thirty. What had he been doing at Michigan? It was clear to Nina that he was an Orthodox Jew. The Hebrew diploma, the beard, the name—everything spelled Ortho. It was out of character for an Ortho to go to law school at Michigan. Most Orthos went to Columbia, if they got in. That way they could still go home for Shabbos dinner and digest Mama's chicken soup along with the Talmudic complexities of contract law.

Nina had also gone out of town to law school, but there had been no Orthos in her class. When she came back to New York for her bar review course, she was shocked. The huge ballroom at the Statler Hilton, where the class had been held, was filled with yarmulkes. The men sat intently bent over their books for hours, frozen in that cramped position. At the break they often ran up to the lecturer to argue some obscure point. Or stayed at their table and argued it among themselves. They never peed. Nina, on the other hand, often spent the break plus the entire second half of the class across the street at Macy's. What really made Nina jealous, more than the Ortho attention span, was the huge shopping bags filled with food these guys brought with them. While Nina was kicking the vending machine, trying to extract her peanut butter crackers, they would be unwrapping whole roast chickens and fresh rye bread.

So what had this guy been doing in Ann Arbor? He didn't wear a yarmulke now, but she bet he did five years ago. She tried to picture Judah Lev walking past the football stadium, surrounded by farmboys and braless coeds. In trying to picture the scene, she puzzled over how tall he was. Seated behind his desk, he looked about five-two. That meant he must be five-six. Whenever Nina thought a man was about five-two he always turned out to be exactly her height—five-six.

Judah Lev rose to shake her hand. "How do you do?" he said, quite formally. He was five-six.

"Thanks so much for taking the time to see me," Nina said. It only took three phone calls and twenty minutes of hocking you to get into your holy sanctuary of an office, she thought. These damn prosecutors, they all had God complexes.

"What can I do for you?"

Nina looked him over again. Actually he wasn't bad looking. He had a fine specimen of a beard. And he wore one of those blue and white striped shirts that Nina always found sexy. They reminded her of pajamas, which reminded her of bed.

"Well, as we discussed on the phone…" Nina launched into the saga of Mrs. Gross and the cockroach powder. He was definitely looking at her tits. Granted he was listening, but his eyes kept making breast contact. Nina was used to men staring at her breasts. For one thing, she lived in New York. Also, they were pretty big. Not Dolly Partonesque or anything, but big. And she had such lousy legs that she tended to dress in a way that drew one's attention upward. The attention often stopped at chest level. Sometimes this made her feel violated, when the tit-starer was creepy or revolting. But sometimes it was okay. She found it hard to be outraged when she was eliciting looks of approval, since Lord knew Nina's life—like nearly everyone else's, she suspected—was little more than a constant quest for approval.

As Nina continued to explain her suspicions about Mrs. Gross's death, Judah Lev alternated between eye and breast contact. She was wearing a purple dress that she had considered quite sedate when she got dressed that morning. It had a high cowl neck and modestly long sleeves. Well, maybe the jersey knit fabric was a little clingy. She faked a watch-checking move and gave her breasts the once-over. You could make out a slight suggestion of a nipple. She really should have worn something a bit more substantial. She felt a pang of guilt, which quickly turned into a stab of righteous indignation. Horny little bastard, thought Nina. She wondered if he was married. It was hard to tell with these Ortho guys, since they didn't always wear wedding rings, which were mandatory among the Upper West Side progressive-lawyer crowd that Nina was used to dealing with. Well, at least he was up-front about his tit-staring. She hated the weasely guys who snuck a peek while you were rummaging around in your purse for a tissue.

When Nina finished her discourse, Judah Lev moved his eyes upward and gazed steadily into hers. "Well, I'm certainly not going to dismiss your theories out of hand," he said. "You're clearly an articulate and intelligent lady, and I would do the people of the state of New York a great disservice if I were not to at least think about what's gone on here."

His use of the word lady startled Nina. In her experience

there was only one kind of man under fifty who could use the word lady without sounding like an asshole. They were the ones who usually preceded the word lady with lovely, and they were often black. If they weren't black, they did quite a bit of coke and had no trouble getting laid. Did this little Ortho spend his non-Shabbos nights snorting and fucking? She had to admit that he had used the word with great aplomb. On him it sounded good. Was it possible that her nipples were standing up just the tiniest bit?

"I'll tell you what's gone on here," she said, pulling her attention back to the subject at hand. "A murder."

"Perhaps." He played with his beard.

He was making her extremely uncomfortable. These Orthos always seemed so omniscient. Nina felt that way about most minority groups. They always seemed to know something she didn't know. Gays, blacks, Hispanics, even children, seemed wiser to her. All the groups other people dismissed as inferior. The Senegalese street vendors seemed the wisest of all.

To regain her composure, she tried going on the offensive. "How come you went all the way out to Michigan to law school?" she asked.

"It was the best school that I got into." He seemed imperturbable.

Did that mean he didn't get into Columbia? Or was Michigan higher ranked than Columbia? It was the kind of thing she had difficulty keeping straight. She had managed to remember the top five, but hadn't quite ranked them in order when she pounced. "So are you going to prosecute this case? I'd like to know as soon as possible."

"Why?" he asked. "Are you planning on taking your business elsewhere?" He had a point there. "Why don't you give me a few days to think this over? I'll get in touch with you as soon as I've made a decision." He stood and shook her hand.

Yes, those were her nipples standing up, and not just the tiniest bit, either. And that was her home phone number she was giving him. Well, after all, it was so hard to reach her at the office.

ααα

"I'm interested," said Judah Lev when he called her at home the next day.

In what? thought Nina. My tits or my murder? "Would you like me to drop off the powder samples at your office?"

"I'm interested in having dinner with you." Well, that answered that.

"You're not interested in my cockroach powder?"

"After careful consideration I've concluded that we lack sufficient evidence to investigate this matter further. But it would show great kindness on your part to give me the pleasure of seeing you again."

This guy has a hell of a nerve, she thought. Meanwhile, in the back of her mind she noted Judah Lev's pronunciation of the word *kindness*. There it was, that telltale glottal stop between the *d* and the *n* among his otherwise flawless pronunciation. It was always present in the speech of people who had learned Yiddish as their first language. She could always tell. The problem with her foolproof method of detection was that there weren't too many words that afforded such clues. There was *kindness* and *greatness* and *lateness* and *Aetna Life Insurance* and not much else. So Nina wasn't able to test people all that often. She had gotten lucky with *kindness*. So Judah Lev was the real thing, not some hippie who had joined up with the Crown Heights Hasidim as his latest cult.

Here she was again, having a tremendously difficult time keeping her mind on her murder. "You mean to tell me you believe that no crime has been committed?" she asked, adding extra indignation to compensate for her wandering attention.

"I would say that it's improbable. But your theory shows great imagination and I admire women with imagination. It's a quality sadly lacking in many people I meet."

Fuck this condescending paternalistic asshole. Who was he to give her an SAT score in imagination? She had already placed herself in the 99th percentile, thank you very much. On the other hand, she was a sucker for anyone who could comfortably use phrases like "sadly lacking" and "great kindness," with or without a glottal stop. The kids she had grown up with used phrases like "boss, man" and then, later, "groovy." "Groovy" metamorphosed into "far out" and then took a sudden swerve into the pretentious "excellent." So when Judah Lev told her that her consent to have dinner with him would be a "great kindness," she melted.

It was hard, when you were the kind of person who had spent your adolescence locked in your bedroom reading Jane Austen, not to spend the rest of your life searching for someone who spoke early-nineteenth-century King's English. Of course, when Nina finally got to spend some time in England and realized that it was actually an island full of dimwits who watched dart tournaments and quiz shows with sheepdogs as contestants on television, she was sorely disappointed. But she never stopped her search for someone who could turn a phrase as well as Austen's Mr. Darcy. Funny that this little Ortho was coming so close.

Did she want to have dinner with Judah Lev? Well, there were a number of problems with that idea, despite his silver tongue and whatever uses he might be able to put it to. First of all, there was Grant. Nina and Grant had never decided whether dating other people was cheating or not. The fact was that they both studiously avoided the topic of monogamy. It was clear that they both strayed, so it wasn't really cheating. But they had been a couple, in their own way, for so long now that Nina couldn't help torturing herself with guilt whenever she wandered off. She suspected Grant felt the same way. It was a system that seemed to work well for both of them.

Then there was the height-age-religion factor. Nina had certainly gone out with a wide range of men in her time. There had been the year when she couldn't bear to look at anybody white. And there had also been the Chinese college football player, the diminutive professor of Slavic languages, the twenty-three-year-old law student who had worked for her one summer. But every time she embarked upon one of these affairs, an image kept recurring. The image of a bride and groom standing before a rabbi. The groom was an appropriate six inches taller and two years older than the bride. And the rabbi was one who would only marry a Jew to another Jew. So despite Nina's wildly open-minded streak to men in practice, she had a theoretical narrow-minded streak. And as her friends married men who were shorter, younger, or not Jewish, she quietly noted it.

Now here was Judah Lev. Definitely younger. Maybe a shade shorter. And, for all intents and purposes, a different religion. For what did Nina know from Orthodox Judaism?

She had a vague recollection of her grandfather, who was the president of his Orthodox congregation in the Bronx. She could picture him in shul, tallised and yarmulked, though the image was a distant one, since she'd had to watch from the women's section in the balcony. But he had been clean-shaven and she couldn't recall ever seeing tefillin wrapped around his arms or ziziths peeking out from beneath his jacket.

Besides, Ida had practically forbidden the girls from discussing religion around their grandparents to avoid conflict. It was Ida's conflict, though, and of course it was unavoidable. And unavoidably conveyed to Nina. Ida wanted her parents to be able to pretend that their granddaughters weren't spending their Friday nights eating barbecued spareribs. Nina was extra careful when she was little, painstakingly deleting all conversational references to Judaism in the presence of her grandparents, for fear of where they might lead. Laura always thought Nina's hypersensitivity was ridiculous. She would chase Nina around the room threatening to tell them about yesterday's BLTs. Once Laura had sat on the toilet in her grandparents' house screaming "Pork chops" at the top of her lungs while Nina hid in the bedroom. Nina still carried a residual sense of discomfort around observant Jews. As if her little sister were inside of her waiting to scream "Pork chops" and bring the wrath of God down upon her.

Nina tried to imagine having dinner with Judah Lev. What was wrong with this picture? Well, he wouldn't look quite right at the end of a pair of chopsticks at Empire Szechuan, Nina's usual haunt. Where did these people go on dates? The kosher deli on Seventy-second Street? What kind of a date was that? A split of champagne and a side of kasha varnishkes? And would she be able to talk to this man? It was one thing to get a cheap thrill out of "great kindness." It was another to keep the conversation going for hours on end. Nina often worried about whether she would have anything to say in social situations. Her fears were generally viewed as ridiculous, since she rarely shut up. But she had been an introverted kid and maintained she was still shy. When she walked into a party she pressed her fingernails into the palms of her hands hard enough to leave little crescent moon indentations. Would a date with Judah Lev leave her with permanently damaged palms?

And she couldn't even begin to imagine what his sexual story might be. Did he do it through holes in the bedsheets? Did he do it at all? And what was he doing asking her out, anyway? He knew she wasn't an Ortho. No way, thought Nina, those guys have antennae for that sort of thing. For one thing, the Ortho women all seemed to have the same haircut. The married ones wore wigs that seemed to come in only one style so they were easy to spot. But even the unmarried ones, the singles who stood in front of the Lincoln Square Synagogue on Saturday mornings gossiping and flirting while Nina schlepped her groceries home from the Red Apple next door, had haircuts that looked like the wigs the married ones wore. They must all go to certain haircutters. Like lesbians, who also all seemed to have variations of the same haircut. In fact, Nina had known a woman who cut lesbian hair. She called her business "Public Hair."

Well, Nina's too-long mop didn't qualify as Ortho hair. And she didn't wear Ortho shoes or speak with an Ortho accent, either. Judah Lev must have known she wasn't kosher. Maybe he was married and hot to get some action on the side. Or maybe he was going through a tref phase, the way she had gone through her black phase. Nina liked the idea of being illicit. Most men were so anxious to drag her home to meet their mothers. Especially the Jews. What the hell, she told herself. She was shy but curious. And her curiosity led her around by the nose. Let it lead her into an evening with Judah Lev. Besides, she had just read an article about all these great new kosher wines that were being produced, and she considered it a cultural gap that she had never tried any.

"That would be very nice," Nina said politely. "How's Friday night?" As soon as the words left her mouth she realized her mistake. Friday wasn't exactly a big dating night in the Orthodox community. Why had she said that? Was it an innocent mistake or was she being unconsciously provocative? Even after years of therapy it was hard to tell.

"We'd better make it Thursday," he said.

"Thursday is good." She was glad he hadn't suggested Saturday. Weekends led to Grant conflicts. She tried to confine her outside activities to weeknights. On the other hand, she was insulted he hadn't suggested Saturday. Was he just another one of these single men who thought that seeing a woman on a weekend was tantamount to a lifelong commitment? These days men squirmed and bent over backwards and fabricated trips abroad in order to avoid asking a woman out for Saturday night. Even her friends who seemed to date during the week never had anything to do during the weekend. If it weren't for Grant, she'd probably consider waiting on tables on Saturday nights. It was the best night for tips and it obviously wouldn't conflict with her social calendar. How disheartening it was to think that this social disease had spread into the synagogues.

"I'll make dinner reservations, if it's all right with you," he said.

"Sure. Are we going to eat in one of those trendy new kosher restaurants?" She felt a little embarrassed. It was the first time she had brought up the religion issue. She felt as if she had broached a sensitive topic, as if he were missing a limb and might not want to discuss it.

"Is that what you would like to do?"

"Well, you're kosher, aren't you?" She stuttered slightly on kosher.

"Yes."

"So what are our choices?" She had to stop talking to him as if his religion were a handicap. She might consider it one, but surely he didn't feel that way. They did this stuff by choice, she told herself.

"I'll take care of it," he said.

"Okay." The whole thing made her nervous. When people told her they would take care of it, things never seemed to work out. She called her mother and told her of Judah Lev's decision not to prosecute. "But don't worry," she added. "I'm going to try to get him to change his mind."

"How are you going to do that?" Ida sounded skeptical.

"As a matter of fact, I'm seeing him on Thursday."

"What are you seeing him about?"

"I'm seeing him. Like on a date."

"Well, this is a first," said Ida. "Does he wear a yarmulke?"

"I don't think so. Not in the office, at any rate. But that might just be for professional purposes. After all, he is a prosecutor. It's tricky enough arguing in front of a jury. You don't need a yarmulke adding to your problems."

Ida felt her mouth twisting downward. She knew without looking in the mirror that her mother's smirk had taken over her face. The first time she had caught sight of that familiar grimace on her own face, she was shocked. Now she was used to it. But really, why be so judgmental about this? Ida prided herself on her open-mindedness. While other mothers hocked their kids about choosing the right career, the right spouse, the right piece of real estate, Ida always maintained that she just wanted her girls to be happy.

But the truth was that Ida would probably have preferred Nina to go out with just about anyone other than an Orthodox Jewish man. Even the high school dropout truck driver Nina dug up in the Midwest hadn't set off such a smirk. Actually, Ida had found him somewhat interesting. But an Ortho? It made the entire twentieth century seem pointless. Ida's mother in steerage and later in the sweat-shop. Ida working to put herself through Hunter during the depression and later to put Nina through law school. Nina pumping herself up every day to do battle with the forces of evil in housing court. So that she could go out with a man who thanked God every morning he wasn't born a woman?

"Have a good time," said Ida and hung up.

15

"**Y**OU WANT TRENDY, we'll get trendy." Judah Lev perused the wine list. "How about Baron Jaquabe de Herzog zinfandel 1984? It's from California."

"Sounds good." Nina felt as though she were traveling. And while visiting other cultures, she liked to immerse herself fully. In Greece she had always had a bottle of retsina with her meal, even though it tasted like turpentine. In Spain she ate flan for dessert, even though it looked like snot. In Holland she always put mayonnaise on her french fries, despite the caloric effect. Canadian french fries were less fattening, since there she used vinegar, though it made them taste like hell. And here she was in a modern Orthodox restaurant. Which of course called for a bottle of modern Orthodox wine.

Nina looked around. You couldn't really tell. It seemed like an ordinary French restaurant. Only the yellow color of the stuff in the butter crock and the large number of yarmulkes gave it away. Judah Lev was one of the crowd. He hadn't been wearing a yarmulke when he picked her up, but he had slipped one on before they entered the restaurant, explaining that he covered his head while he ate.

"So what are we doing here?" she asked. When she wasn't sure how to initiate a conversation, she resorted to asking extremely vague questions, subject to many different interpretations. It was like a Rorschach test. Throw something out to see where the other person chose to lead.

But Judah Lev would have none of it. "What do you mean?" The ball was quickly back on her side of the court. And she didn't have the nerve to start in with "What do you think I mean?" Between his Talmudic background and her decade of therapy, they'd be volleying all night.

He was staring at her collarbones. Nina had purposely worn a loose sweater. A half-hour of tit-staring was one thing, but an entire evening could make one very nonplussed. But she had worn a sweater with a neckline low enough to show off her prominent collarbones and long neck. It always amazed her that she could have such a long neck and such short legs. Sometimes it seemed as though her neck was longer than her legs.

She decided to plunge right in. "Aren't you sort of dating outside of your faith?"

"You mean to tell me that Nina Fischman is not a Jew?"

"Well, sure I'm a Jew. But not exactly your kind of Jew. I mean, don't you consider Jews like me worse than goyim?"

"Worse in what way? Worse basketball players? Yes, you make worse basketball players than the goyim."

Jesus, why did she ever think she could handle this guy? The combination of Orthodox and prosecutor was impossible. She didn't want to spend the evening being crossexamined. She would try putting him on direct. "Are you married?" she asked.

"No."

"Do you want to get married?"

"Yes."

"Do you want to marry an Orthodox woman?"

"Yes."

"Do you consider dating a means of effectuating marriage?"

"Of course."

"So what are we doing here?"

"Having dinner. Showing you that all kosher wine isn't Manischewitz. And that all yeshiva boys aren't pale little worms."

"So I take it that this cross-cultural experience is primarily for my edification?"

"Do I strike you as the kind of man who devotes his evenings to the poor and needy?" Judah Lev had moved his gaze upward from her collarbones to the vicinity of her throat. He looked at her hungrily, the kind of look Nina generally reserved for Chinese food.

"Well," said Nina, her hand modestly fluttering to her neck, "I don't know how far you carry the concept of mitzvah."

"'Mitzvah' is the wrong word. Sex is the right word. That's what I'm getting out of this evening. Sex." He tore his eyes away from her throat and stared into hers.

"How do you know?"

"My dear Nina, don't you know we're having sex already? Seeing you, hearing you, smelling you. To me, that's having sex with you. I don't need to touch you."

He was making her extremely aroused and extremely nervous. "Well, that's one way to deal with the contemporary crisis of sexually transmitted disease." It was no time for sarcasm, she knew, but she was too nervous to help herself.

"Nina, let me make something clear. You do not need to worry about sexually transmitted diseases with me. For two reasons. The first is that I am not a carrier. I am, in fact, a virgin. The second is that I will remain a virgin until I marry. Therefore we will not be having sexual intercourse."

The waiter chose that moment to bring the wine. Waiters always seemed to show up at the exact moment that someone at the table was saying "sexual intercourse."

The wine tasted pretty good. Like all white zinfandels, it was sweetish. Funny, Nina thought, how these things went in and out of style. When she was in college, there wasn't much drinking going on. Alcohol was considered suburban and reactionary. Men who played golf drank. But occasionally, to supplement their marijuana, Nina and her friends would indulge in a sweet wine. She could remember getting sick on Boone's Farm Strawberry Hill at several rock concerts. By the time Nina got to law school, everyone was already drinking sophisticated dry chardonnays. Later, when she started dating black men, they often showed up at her door clutching a bottle of Riunite or Taylor Lake Country White, sweet enough to rival Manischewitz. Now, years later, came this white zinfandel business. In the midst of "the drier the better," people were flocking to these sweetish blush wines. It was all very unpredictable. Thank God for the Living section of the *Times*, so you could keep track of these things.

Well, the wine wasn't the only thing blushing at the dinner table. Nina had turned bright red at Judah Lev's pronouncement that "we will not be having sexual intercourse." He did not say it unkindly. In fact, he said it gently and instructively, the way he had told her he would be picking her up at eight. What do you say to someone who has just told you that you will not be having sexual intercourse? She had never been in that situation before. It was like being a teenage boy in the fifties with blueballs. At least she didn't have to wonder how this date was going to end. It was actually sort of a relief. She found herself becoming increasingly provocative. The way you never want something until you can't have it. By the end of the meal she had aroused herself into a frenzy.

After dinner they walked down Columbus Avenue staring into store windows and at each other. When they got to her corner she said, "You can come up, you know, without having sexual intercourse."

"I think I'll save the invitation for another time. Is that all right with you?"

"Sure. But you could at least kiss me good night."

He kissed her in a way that you can only get kissed when all you're getting is kissed. Like in the old movies with no sex, just kissing. Kissing as a sex act unto itself. He was a good kisser.

She called in her report the next morning. "So did you get him to change his mind?" asked Ida.

"Well, the subject never came up."

"What do you mean, the subject never came up? A murder has been committed. It's your duty to see to it that it's vigorously prosecuted."

"It just didn't seem like the right time and place to start hocking him about pursuing an investigation," Nina said. The truth was that during her evening with Judah Lev, Nina had completely forgotten about Mrs. Gross and the digitalis traces. It was only now, as she called her mother, that she even remembered that one of the items on her agenda, in addition to the kosher wine, had been to encourage him to look further into the old lady's death.

How had this come about? For one thing, she had felt mildly possessed. Ever since Judah Lev had shown up on her doorstep in his gray pullover, she hadn't been herself. Even his pullover had aroused her. It was hand knit by, as it turned out, his mother. The wool was charcoal gray and had interesting heathery flecks of purple in it. And gloriously fat, intricate cables. Nina was a connoisseur of cables. She liked wide ones, twelve stitches across at a minimum. Judah's looked to be at least twenty. And convoluted, crossing every which way, textural.

Like his mind. She also was, of course, a connoisseur of minds. Nina viewed conversation like a theatrical production. She needed several subplots going in order to sustain her interest. She also required dramatic tension, plot points, and surprise developments. Judah Lev was a master. All through dinner he had managed to keep three conversational balls in the air, switching from one subject to another whenever the dramatic tension lagged even the slightest bit. And subtly suffusing the entire scene with sex.

The conversation had been sexy, if not directly about sex. For example, he had really gotten to Nina when he told her what great skin she had. Nina rarely thought about her skin.

While she was growing up, all her friends were trying desperately to make their hair flip and their stomachs flat and their eyeliner go on straight. But skin care in the Bronx went no further than using Clearasil and popping pimples. Once her pimples subsided, she stopped thinking about her skin. It wasn't something you continued to attack ferociously, like your weight. It was just there. Every now and then someone, usually a woman considerably older and wealthier than she, would allude to her lovely skin. Nina was always pleasantly surprised. But, to her, skin care remained the province of the rich, something you could attend to when everything else was out of the way. An upscale hobby, like collecting Victorian silver or knowing about cognac.

And most men went for the more obvious. Their compliments were confined to topics like her tits. Sometimes they mentioned her hair or eyes. But Judah Lev was the first man who had ever told her she had great skin. Nina thought that displayed an admirable depth of awareness. Like noticing which pieces of classical music were used in a movie soundtrack.

She had wisecracked, dredging up a line from an old Woody Allen movie. "Thank you," she had said. "It covers my whole body." And in fact that described exactly the state of arousal she was in. Some men made your nipples get erect and some made you so wet you had to change your underpants. But Judah Lev aroused her skin. She had a heightened awareness all over her body that evening that had lasted into the next day.

"Next time," she told her mother. "I promise that next time I see him I'll discuss Mrs. Gross with him. If there is a next time," Nina added quickly, anticipating her mother's question.

For Nina had no idea of what was on the agenda. Usually she could predict the next move. A lot of men said, "I enjoyed myself very much. I'd like to do this again soon. I'll call you in a few days." Those were easy. They'd call by Wednesday at the latest, by which time Nina had already decided that she never wanted to see them again. Then there were the sexual conquistadores. They acted very big on getting laid. But it never seemed to matter whether or not they actually talked Nina into bed. Either way, they would call erratically, at odd times. It was clear that their sexual schedules were so complicated that she would always be filling in the gaps. In the third category were the cheaters. They were often interesting and attractive, but Nina could tell there was something wrong.

A wife, a girlfriend, or sometimes a boyfriend in the picture. These men were never heard from again. Except sometimes a year later when they had resolved their difficulties and Nina could barely remember who they were. Once a married man named Steven called her a full two years after their only date. "Hi, it's Steven," he had said. Nina wasn't the type to say "Steve who?" Not because it was rude, but because she considered it a challenge to rack her brain and figure out the last name of the person on the other end of the line. Nina, being a typical New York Jew born in the fifties, knew at least two dozen Stevens. There were Stevens at work, in her building, on both her mother's and father's side of the family, and many of her friends were dating or married to men named Steven. She finally gave up. It turned out that this Steven had gotten divorced in the past year. She remembered having been attracted to him at the time she went out with him. But now she had to pass. She decided anyone who could call after two years and say "Hi, it's Steven" must be psychotic.

Nina had once read an interview with a CEO who said the secret to success in business was the ability to withstand uncertainty. Well, that was certainly true about dating. She tried to cultivate her ability to withstand uncertainty, but it wore her out. Especially in addition to all the uncertainty she had to withstand in the courtroom. Sometimes Nina thought that the combination of dating and litigating was too much for one girl to take.

Judah Lev fell into the cheating category. But instead of cheating on a woman he was cheating on God. Nina had never encountered this situation before, so it was hard to predict his next move. But she was getting a certain amount of pleasure from the uncertainty. It added a tangible dimension, like a scent. She was enjoying it the way she enjoyed reading a really good Agatha Christie mystery with a lot of lush details about French windows and kippers for breakfast. This romance had atmosphere.

16

NINA'S NEW ROMANCE was interrupted by the Memorial Day weekend. She had been feeling pretty remote from Grant the past few weeks, but he hadn't seemed to notice. Spring was their busy season, since the evictions that resulted from rent withholding during the heating season were just coming onto the court calendar. He was preoccupied, working around the clock. Nina and Grant always spent Memorial Day weekend at Terry and Steve's country house in Columbia County. Nina liked it up there. It was less glitzy than the Hamptons, more like a northern extension of the Upper West Side. The Upper West Side the way it used to be, before blond people moved there. Although even Columbia County was getting its share of blond people lately. This year Nina noticed that Taconic Orchards was carrying pesto in a tube.

Steve and Terry's house was in the northern part of the county, so the drive up the Taconic Parkway was well over two hours. Since she sat in the back seat and was prone to car sickness, Nina was extremely glad when they pulled into the driveway. The big old house had plenty of guest bedrooms. Nina and Grant always used the one that faced west. The house was on a hill and late in the day you could watch the sun set over the Catskills.

At breakfast on Saturday morning Terry perused the local

papers, scanning for auctions. She and Steve were addicted, engaged in the never-ending search for the perfect Hoosier cabinet and yet another slightly frayed wedding band quilt. The country house afforded them the opportunity to buy overstuffed furniture and big oak antiques. Their tiny city apartment was all compact high-tech efficiency. A tube of chrome and a sling of leather was a chair. A slab of glass was a table and two strips of black steel bolted together was a lamp. You couldn't sit comfortably there for too long, but Terry and Steve never needed to. It was more like a landing pad than a home for them. Weeknights were spent in the office working late or in Chinese restaurants. Domestic comforts were confined to the weekend.

Grant usually skipped the auctions. He was uninterested in furniture and preferred to stay home and work his way through the stack of periodicals and court-related documents he always brought with him. Nina, though also uninterested in furniture, loved auctions. They were like theater and shopping combined. And since she rarely had the energy to do either in the city, country auctions filled a void. Apparently they filled a void for a lot of city folks, for lately the auction barns had been packing them in. On Saturdays the Chatham Skaterama looked as if it were hosting a Bank Street nursery school PTA meeting.

Nina was especially looking forward to an auction, since she was agitated and too jumpy to sit still. Especially when she was alone with Grant. She had been through this before. Over the years both Nina and Grant had wandered off and wandered back again without creating a fuss. But she was finding it harder to keep two things going simultaneously. Her thirty-fifth birthday loomed large. She felt a great deal older now than she had in the days when she could flit between men without even taking out her diaphragm.

"No auctions until tomorrow," said Terry, after a thorough search.

"What do you guys want to do today?" asked Steve, who was

at the griddle making a second batch of French toast. That was the great thing about the country. It made men want to cook.

"Nothing," said Grant. "I brought some work with me."

"I need to do some gardening," said Terry. When she wasn't at an auction, she spent most of her time in the garden, like the dutiful Italian daughter she was in some ways. Every year she cultivated more and more varieties of basil.

"I've got to go over to Agway, and then I'm going to tackle that gutter that's falling down," said Steve.

"I think I'll cook something ambitious," said Nina. Following some pointlessly complicated recipe could be soothing. She made her way over to the cookbooks and started to flip through them, looking for something she would never attempt under normal circumstances. She found a calzone recipe, with yeast and dough and fresh herbs and thinly sliced pepperoni, that looked as if it would consume the entire day. It also required a shopping expedition, which suited her purposes.

That afternoon, as she chopped and kneaded, she relaxed a bit. Every now and then she would trot out the thought of Judah Lev and give herself a little thrill. It was funny, that sudden feeling of arousal that hit her in her stomach. She was at the stove sautéing onions when Steve and Grant walked into the kitchen.

"Whatever happened with that D.A.?" Steve asked. It took her by surprise, since she had just been imagining Judah Lev standing behind her at the stove with his hands inside her sweater.

"Nothing." She sounded more than a bit defensive.

"Did you give him the powder samples?" Steve had been following the cockroach caper with great interest.

"Yeah, but he seemed unimpressed."

"Nina's going to meet with him again. She's not giving up easily," Grant said proudly. Nina had vowed to Grant to wage a never-ending campaign—just to cover herself in case she let any

Judah Lev references slip. Grant had taken it as a sign that Nina was tapping into a new enthusiasm for the law and a rebirth of the fighting spirit that she had maintained for about her first twenty minutes in housing court. Now, he thought, maybe she would be more willing to share his passion. Or at least not look at her watch every time he mentioned one of his clients. It made Nina squirm to think how her lie had made him so happy.

Grant's enthusiasm was infectious, at least as far as Steve was concerned. "You've got to see this thing through," he said. "Remember that a D.A. is little more than a bureaucrat. He's there to shove paper across his desk. In order to get him to stop shoving paper and actually take some action, you've got to be more than persuasive. You've got to present him with a case that is practically a *fait accompli*. Which means doing most of the work for him so that all he has to do is finish it off and take the credit."

"It's like being in front of a judge," Grant said. "You know how they work. They don't want to have to do any research or hard thinking. Give them a brief that can easily be turned into an opinion and you're in good shape. I'm sure it's the same with the D.A.'s office."

"He didn't seem to think a crime had been committed," Nina said as she layered the onions over the bottom calzone crust.

"He needs more evidence." Steve was getting excited. "What if we gave him a pattern?"

"You mean bring Mrs. Kahn into it?" said Grant.

"Right. Her apartment hasn't been checked for traces of digitalis, has it?"

"It hadn't occurred to me." Nina shrugged and reached for the pepperoni.

"What if you went back to Kahn's apartment and found the same substance in her kitchen? Wouldn't that get him off his ass?"

Nina nodded as she thought about Judah Lev's ass. It was a little flat. Actually all male asses seemed a little flat to her since she had stopped dating black men.

"Steve's right," said Grant. "You should make an appointment with that broker to see Mrs. Kahn's apartment and take some samples."

Nina carefully overlapped pepperoni slices in a large spiral. It was true. She had let herself get sidetracked by romance. She would call her mother and tell her to get out some more suppository containers. Ida surely had an endless supply.

The calzone was a big hit that night. Terry and Steve brought out two bottles of red from a local winery. Grant abstained, claiming red wine gave him a headache.

Nina rolled her eyes. "He's impossible," she said. "A real drip. Are we going to go through this on my birthday again? Last year we had take-out Chinese food and orange juice."

"What do you want from me?" Grant said. "You want me to get dressed up in a smoking jacket and sip martinis and dance like Fred Astaire?"

Nina imagined a smoking jacket over Grant's dark green BVD T-shirt. The same one he had worn as a University of Wisconsin freshman. "A cheap bottle of champagne would do."

"When's your birthday?" asked Terry.

"A week from tomorrow."

"Why don't we drive down a little early next Sunday and have dinner with you and Grant? We'll go someplace nice."

"Someplace with a liquor license?" Nina asked hopefully.

"Absolutely. We'll pick the place. It'll be a surprise. Does that sound okay, Steve?"

"Sounds great."

Nina's spirits perked up. It would be more fun. These days when she and Grant went out to dinner alone they usually brought something to read.

17

WHEN NINA GOT BACK TO TOWN there was a message from Judah Lev on her machine. The first answering machine message was critical. You could always predict the future based on those first few syllables. She had been the first of her friends to own one, having inherited an early model from Ken when he upgraded. Now every unmarried woman in New York had one. The really hard core had call waiting.

Nina thought back to all those messages left during past years. She remembered both the promising and the disappointing ones. She had learned to stay away from lousy Bogart imitations and anything that started with "You might not remember me" or "It's four o'clock in the morning." Slurred speech was also not propitious. The best ones were the straightforward ones that adequately combined humility with self-assuredness. Judah Lev's was pretty good. "Nina, I'm going out of town for the weekend. Perhaps you are also." She admired people who could say "perhaps" instead of "maybe" without sounding pretentious. Nina could never quite make it work. "I'll call you as soon as I get back."

And he did. He reached her in the office on Tuesday. "Are you busy on Sunday?"

She was being elevated to the weekend. Her stomach did that funny flip again. "Sunday's my birthday," Nina said. "My thirty-fifth. I already have plans for the evening."

"If it's your birthday, we'll have to celebrate. What about the afternoon? We can have a picnic in the Brooklyn Botanic Gardens. The cherry blossoms are gone, but I think the lilacs will be out. I'll bring lunch. Weinstock makes a chardonnay that I think you'll like."

There was little that Judah Lev could have said that would have made her happier. Nina had spent her entire life trying to get men to go on picnics. Picnics seemed like the height of romance to her. But men always seemed to view them as point-less preoccupations. With bugs, rain, and potential food poison-ing from rancid mayonnaise. Here was a picnic thrown right into her lap. And on her birthday, no less. With wine. What could be better? It occurred to Nina that it might be a bit undignified to spend her thirty-fifth birthday running from one man to another. Would it be something that would haunt her in middle age? That she would regret forever? Possibly. She would see.

Sunday was one of those glorious days when Nina kept catching herself humming "I like New York in June, how about you?" It was a time of year when it was easy to be corny. June was such a relief. The basic concept of spring in the Northeast was a fraud. Not like in the South, where it was a slow, gentle process with something new blooming every week. In New York people started getting their hopes up in February. Not because they actually expected it to get warmer, but to ward off their suicidal depression. All through March they walked around saying "Just wait. Hang on a little bit longer." They invariably spent April prematurely taking the lining out of their raincoat and then buttoning it back in. By May everyone was extremely crabby. Then one day a couple of weeks into the month the temperature would shoot up from forty to eighty, sending the city into a tailspin. Eight million people would all rush to the dry cleaner with their linen skirts and khaki pants. It was very disconcerting. By the time June came, the city had calmed down. The women had bought new knee-high stockings and remembered that their peach sweater looked best with their plaid skirt. The men had the buttons sewn back on their summer suits. The office buildings and health clubs had worked out the kinks in their air-conditioning systems.

Judah Lev showed up with a shopping bag. It had been too much to hope for a wicker picnic basket. At least the shopping bag was paper, not plastic. It was from Macy's in that awful color that reminded Nina of liver. Why did they continue to produce those monstrosities year after year while Bloomingdale's made bags worthy of a museum retrospective?

When he picked her up at her apartment he kissed her the way he had at the end of their first date. It made her remember how wonderful kissing was on its own. After all these years with Grant, it was rare that he ever kissed her without his cock being inside her.

Judah Lev had borrowed a car for the occasion. They parked in the Brooklyn Museum parking lot and he led her to a spot near the lilac arbor, which was in bloom. He clearly knew the park well. The blanket he had brought for them to sit on was not your typical picnic schmatta. Nina was used to old Indian cotton throws recycled from dorm rooms. Or Marimekko sheets in discontinued patterns. Judah Lev had what once had been a chenille bedspread. She hadn't seen one like it since her grandmother went into the nursing home. It was sweet really. Sort of Victorian.

He unpacked the Weinstock along with a spread of cheeses and a pasta salad. The chardonnay was pretty good. Nina downed a couple of glasses quickly to calm her nerves.

Judah Lev watched with amusement while she guzzled the wine. "So this is a big birthday for you, isn't it?" he said. "When the alarm goes off on your biological clock?"

"Oh, please. It's been ticking so loud lately I can't hear anything else."

"So what's the problem? You're beautiful, you're smart. You could get married next week if you wanted to."

"I don't know. All I know is that I'm thirty-five and still running around like it was 1968. I have a boyfriend who's a superannuated hippie and a rental apartment the size of my sister's laundry room. I have clients who bring me documents with cockroach carcasses pressed in them. And here I am getting drunk on kosher wine in Brooklyn with an Orthodox Jew before I run off to meet my boyfriend who makes me seethe with resentment because we never do anything except eat Chinese food." They had never discussed Grant before. She felt relieved to have come clean, although she got the feeling it probably didn't much matter. She finished her glass of wine.

"Are you drunk?" Judah Lev asked.

"I think so."

"Good." He pressed his mouth to hers as they lay back onto the blanket. "So soft," he said.

Nina felt soft all over as her body came up against the contours of his. Her breasts felt like down pillows against the firmness of his chest. And the hardness of his cock poked into the soft roundness of her thighs. Heterosexuality was a wonderful thing, she thought, as her nipples shot up toward the blue Brooklyn sky. Soft and hard. It was thrilling to feel so soft. I'll never go near another Nautilus machine, she swore, as her lips parted and his tongue probed the soft inside of her mouth.

18

NINA'S BIRTHDAY DINNER turned out to be a disappointment. Terry and Steve phoned to say their car had broken down and they were staying upstate overnight to have it fixed. Grant tried to make it up to her by bringing champagne and flowers, but the champagne was of a cheap pink variety and the flowers were carnations dyed blue. The effect was dismal. They ended up going out to a Thai restaurant, which was supposed to be more special than Chinese since the entrees cost a dollar more. But lemongrass and peanut sauce weren't doing it for Nina. Her mind kept drifting back to the chenille bedspread.

Her mother called her in the office on Monday. "I tried you yesterday, but I couldn't get you in. I think you forgot to turn on your machine. How was your birthday?"

"Pretty busy."

"Have you seen that D.A. lately?"

"Uh-huh."

"Has he said anything about the case?"

"We didn't really discuss it."

"What did you discuss?"

"I don't quite remember. Listen, Ma, Steve had an idea."

Now that the shock of her birthday had worn off, Nina was ready to get back down to business.

"Which one is Steve? I can't keep track of your male harem."

"Don't get nasty. Steve is Grant's friend, the one who had the client who lived in the other West Estates apartment."

"Oh, right. What was his idea?"

"He thinks that you and I should go over to Mrs. Kahn's apartment and take samples. If we get digitalis traces there also, we might establish enough of a pattern to convince the D.A. to investigate further."

"It's a good idea," said Ida. "We certainly have nothing to lose. I'll call Patricia White and schedule another viewing. When's good for you?"

"Any night this week except Thursday. I'm meeting with a tenant group on rent strike at seven-thirty. And of course I have group on Tuesday, as usual."

"I'll see what I can do. I hope the apartment is still on the market. It was a real beauty. I wouldn't be surprised if somebody bought it already."

Ida arranged for them to see the apartment at seven that evening and by the time Nina arrived at her mother's, Patricia White was already there. This time her three-inch-heeled suede pumps were purple. Her suit was a slightly bluer purple. The shoes and suit were different enough colors to make the ensemble a slightly risky proposition. But it worked beautifully. Nina wondered if the woman had schlepped around the suit as she shopped for the shoes or vice versa. Or maybe she didn't have to schlepp around either one, she just knew. Patricia White was a genius, thought Nina. It was too bad she couldn't make a living out of shoe matching, because she certainly didn't know that much about apartments. This time, as Ida scurried around scooping, Nina tried to engage White in a discussion about thermal pane windows.

"You know I really miss the divided panes they used to have in these old buildings," Nina said. They were in the living room and Ida was in the kitchen.

"These are easy to clean," White said, as if reciting from a brochure. "They flip inside. Let me show you." She started to fumble with the window.

"Never mind, I know what you mean. My mother has the same windows. And I understand all about their cleaning ease and heat-conservation properties. But I can't help but feel they degrade the architectural integrity of the pre-war buildings."

Patricia White shrugged. "Where's your mother?" she said and glanced at her watch.

Nina's mind raced. What would be guaranteed to get this woman's attention? she wondered. "That suit is a real stunner," she said. "What shade would you say it was?"

Patricia White smiled and stopped looking at her watch. She gave Nina her full attention. "I think of it as iris," she said.

"And the shoes?" Nina asked. "They're not really quite iris, are they? They're purpler."

White leaned against the windowsill and extended one of her long limbs. She examined her pump with grave attention for a full half-minute. "Violet?" Nina suggested.

Mrs. White shook her head. "No, I wouldn't say violet. To me, violet suggests something paler. They're really deeper than violet." She was starting to sound almost confident and articulate.

"Lavender?" prompted Nina. She felt as if she had finally made a connection with the woman. When she was a teenager she had read magazine articles that suggested she attempt to talk to boys about football. She thought the idea incredibly stupid at the time and insisted on being true to herself. But here she was trying out the same theory and it was working.

"No, not lavender." White was making eye contact with her

for the first time since they had met. "To me, lavender means something even paler than violet. I would call them…" She paused to let the tension mount: "Amethyst," she finally said.

"Yes, amethyst, definitely," Nina agreed. "What color would you say my skirt is?" This was getting to be fun. "Burgundy?" she suggested.

"No," said White. "It has a bit of brown mixed in."

"Claret?"

"No, claret doesn't suggest the brown, either."

"I guess cranberry doesn't, either."

"No, I would say that your skirt is…" White paused again for dramatic effect. "Maple," she pronounced.

Nina nodded enthusiastically. They moved on to Nina's purse, which they decided was dove. And then on to her sweater, which turned out to be greige. Nina had never heard of greige, but White assured her that the word had been in common usage for years. After all, how else would you describe gray and beige mixed together? Nina was fascinated, despite herself. Eight o'clock came and went and Ida finally had to drag the two of them out of there. Nina walked White to the elevator as they continued to debate whether Nina's watchband was caramel or chestnut.

Ken had agreed to have the samples analyzed, and Ida dropped them off at his office the following day. This time he had a rush put on them and the results were back in twenty-four hours. Ida called Nina on Wednesday. "Guess what?" she said. "Digitalis in the kitchen again."

"Holy shit." Nina sounded shocked. "We're really on to something, aren't we?"

"Of course we are. I thought all I had to do was convince your little bearded friend. I didn't realize I had to convince you, too."

Nina shrugged. "I guess I only half believed it up until now. I'll call Judah Lev right away."

"I don't trust you anymore," said Ida. "You're too easily

distracted. This time I will accompany you to your meeting with Mr. Lev. Please arrange for an appointment."

Nina called Judah Lev right away. "You're meeting my mother," she said.

"I don't think that's such a good idea, Nina."

She listened to him wriggle before she let him off the hook. "You're meeting her for professional purposes only. We've got a new piece of evidence concerning Mrs. Gross's death, and my mother wants to present it to you."

"Certainly. It would be my pleasure." His pomposity was suffused with relief.

"We'll be over tomorrow at five."

They were prompt. Judah Lev kept them waiting a scant five minutes, which was some kind of a record with government lawyers.

Ida was barely seated before she began. "My daughter tells me you're not stupid or lazy. Therefore I am assuming that this meeting will not be a waste of time."

Nina cringed. "A little too harsh, Ma," she said. "I think the man would be more responsive to cordiality."

"Forgive me, Mr. Lev. I was simply attempting to compensate for my daughter's behavior. Which I understand has been overly cordial. And to which you've been very responsive."

He knew when to back off. "What can I do for you?" he asked.

Ida reached into her Channel 13 tote bag. She lined the powder samples up on Judah Lev's desk. "I am convinced that a crime has been committed. If you're agreeable, I will set forth my theory, outlining the facts as I believe they occurred. Please permit me to continue without interruption. I will be as brief as possible."

"By all means. Go ahead." Judah Lev tipped his chair back and leaned his head against the wall, just below his law school diploma.

"I own an apartment at three-nineteen West End Avenue. Until her recent demise, my neighbor in apartment seven-A was Mrs. Bertha Gross. At the time of her death she was eighty-two years old. However, she was of sound health. Mrs. Gross was under the care of a neighborhood physician named Dr. Gerald Weissberg. According to another neighbor, Dr. Weissberg had informed Mrs. Gross that her heart was in excellent condition, and yet she died suddenly last April of cardiac arrest. At the time I assumed it was of natural causes. However, subsequent to her death, I had the occasion to procure several samples of the material used to combat cockroach infestation in Mrs. Gross's apartment. I had the samples chemically analyzed. The material taken from the kitchen contained digitalis, a drug that can induce cardiac arrest when taken internally. These facts have already been brought to your attention by my daughter, have they not?"

"Yes, they have." Judah Lev nodded.

"Well," Ida continued, "I am now in possession of a new set of facts that will conclusively prove that a crime was indeed committed."

"Excuse me, Mrs. Fischman," he said. "Where did you learn to talk that way? Did you have a career as a trial attorney that your daughter didn't tell me about?"

"Young man, there was a time when it was very difficult to obtain a position as a New York City public school teacher. We had to be extremely articulate. We were tested for diction, grammar, and regional accent. The system was staffed by a group of women so well spoken they could have undoubtedly won the"—Ida paused as she glanced at the wall behind Judah Lev—"University of Michigan Law School Moot Court competition," she finished.

"I see." He smiled. "If you're at all typical, I would say that's correct."

"May I now present the new set of facts I previously referred to?"

"Believe me, you have my complete attention."

"As you know, my daughter is an attorney who represents the elderly indigent. She had the occasion to discuss Mrs. Gross's death with a colleague of hers, a Mr. Steven Glass. He informed her that the circumstances surrounding Mrs. Gross's death sounded extremely similar to those of the death of a client of his—Mrs. Etta Kahn of three twenty-two West End Avenue. She died the same month as Mrs. Gross. Therefore, my daughter and I took the liberty of obtaining samples from Mrs. Kahn's apartment also. The samples from her kitchen contained digitalis in an amount similar to that in the sample from the Gross apartment. There is a further link between Mrs. Kahn and Mrs. Gross. Neither of them had purchased their apartments when their buildings converted to cooperatives. They stayed on as non-purchasing tenants, with their tenancy protected by the conversion laws until their death. In both cases the unsold shares allocated to their apartments were subsequently sold to a Netherlands Antilles corporation known as West Estates, N.V. And both apartments had been exterminated by an independent contractor arranged for by the owner. Special arrangements had been made in lieu of using the regular building exterminator. I think only one conclusion can be drawn."

"And what's that?" Judah Lev scribbled something on a notepad.

"The owner of the two apartments poisoned Mrs. Gross and Mrs. Kahn in order to be able to sell the units as vacant and command a high price."

"You've done an excellent investigative job, Mrs. Fischman. There is one area that remains problematic, however. I assume that neither of the old ladies was in the habit of eating cockroach powder."

"I was not acquainted with Mrs. Kahn, but I was familiar with the personal habits of Mrs. Gross. She exhibited no eccentricities of the sort."

"So you see why we still have an evidentiary problem here. It's not enough to go to the grand jury with. But I'll admit that the situation warrants further investigation."

Ida reached back into her Channel 13 tote. "Here is the address and phone number of a Mr. Myron Kaplan. He is the designated managing agent for West Estates. He is an extremely unpleasant man. Unpleasant to a suspicious extent. If it's at all possible, I would like to get that bastard."

"We'll see what we can do," said Judah Lev. But he would say no more. Nina smiled weakly as they exited.

Ida and Nina went across the street to a coffee shop. "So what did you think?" asked Nina as they settled into a booth.

"I can't tell," said Ida. "He seemed to take us seriously, but he certainly hustled us out of his office pretty quickly."

"I meant what did you think about him? Don't you think he's cute?"

"Nina, he hardly has the potential to become a national sex symbol. I mean, Cary Grant he's not."

"Ma, I'm surprised at your lack of imagination. Any moron could be attracted to Cary Grant. Be a little expansive, for chrissakes."

"I'm sorry, but I did not grow up in a time when nerdy little men like Woody Allen and Dustin Hoffman walked off with the leading lady. I predate the era of the antihero."

"But the flip side of that is the worship of the tall, thin blond woman. Where does that leave us?"

"Right where we've always been. Certainly not in front of the camera."

"You give up too easily, Ma. Where would Streisand be if she had your spirit?"

"Teaching school."

"What a waste."

"Actually," said Ida, "I suppose Judah Lev does have a certain appeal. He has big brown eyes and he couldn't keep them off you. But I don't trust him. I think there's a good chance he'll do nothing on this case."

"I'll see what I can get out of him. Although I hate to mix business with pleasure."

Nina thought about the pleasure she was getting out of Judah Lev. It was certainly different from the usual sweaty-bodies-pressed-together-at-three-o'clock-in-the-morning pleasure. It was a small kind of pleasure. A nose pressed against an ear. A finger brushing the inside of a wrist. A smile and then a kiss. All very quiet. No shrieks of ecstasy, no loud breathing or moaning. A perfect June romance. Not too hot. The light yellow-green of spring. Soft breezes. Nothing scorching. What would happen when summer came? Nina couldn't picture Judah Lev in a bathing suit. Or naked, for that matter. She didn't even know whether he had hair on his chest. Not that she had any clear preference. Women she knew seemed to have special requirements as to quantity and configuration of chest hair. Nina could never decide. She tried to picture Judah Lev with and without chest hair. Either way, a blue oxford shirt kept covering him up in her mind.

19

NINA CALLED JUDAH LEV at home that evening. "As a complainant," she said, "I have a right to know how your investigation is proceeding." She said the word complainant to herself several times. She liked the sound of it. She decided to incorporate it into her vocabulary. Next time someone accused her of being a kvetch, she would tell them she was a complainant. It sounded much more hopeful.

"You're not a complainant in the traditional sense," he said. "As the victim of a crime is a complainant."

"I still have a right to know what's going on."

"Only to the extent I deem appropriate. Certainly not to an extent that would interfere with my conducting a successful investigation. I represent the people of the state of New York, not just Nina and Ida Fischman."

"What kind of interference are you afraid of?"

"Your mother seemed a little hot under the collar. Especially the way she talked about Myron Kaplan: 'I'd like to get that bastard.' That was a bit much. I don't want Kaplan getting wind of an investigation. The last thing I need is your mother marching into his office and screaming, 'The D.A.'s gonna get you.'"

So there was an investigation going on. Let it go, Nina told herself. It's in the hands of a professional. It was a familiar plea that never seemed to work. She wished she could be one of those people who could just widen their eyes, say "My lawyer's handling it" or "My brother-in-law is taking care of that," and skip merrily on her way. But Nina never believed anything could successfully occur except under her scrutiny. She wasn't a naturally trusting soul.

Actually the control thing was a little unpredictable. Usually she went nuts at the thought of giving over control. In the passenger seat of a car, she always sat with a map on her lap. The very thought of general anesthesia was enough to make her hysterical. Yet she had no fear of flying. On a plane she yielded willingly. While other people gripped their armrests in panic, she calmly ate her honey-roasted peanuts. She knew that there was nothing she could do to help pilot a plane and was more than happy to sit back and put her life in the hands of Captain WASP with hawklike vision who sat behind the controls.

Could she transfer this feeling to Judah Lev? Could she let him successfully pilot this investigation? What about the relationship? That, too, seemed to be out of her hands. There was something holy about Judah Lev's life which she was reluctant to intrude upon. Apparently there were rules that she had to play by which she didn't really understand.

"I'll take care of it," he said, as if on cue.

"I hate men who tell me they'll take care of it."

"Why?"

"It's paternalistic and indicates a desire to seize control over my life."

"That's ridiculous. Prosecuting this case is what I get paid to do."

"I wasn't just talking about this case." Nina waited to see where this would lead. It was the first time she had initiated a discussion about their relationship, or whatever it was they were having.

"Still nonsense. First of all, I obviously have no desire to seize control of your life. We see each other maybe once a week. What you do with the rest of your time is up to you. Second, I can't help but get the feeling that what you want more than anything is for someone to wrest control of your life from you. Although you make a big show of being an independent woman, it seems to me that you're begging for some direction."

Was she begging for direction? Nina wasn't sure. Part of her felt like a successful career woman with plenty of male companionship who found her life very stimulating. In some ways she had it all. In other ways she had nothing. She was thirty-five, unmarried, childless, conflicted about her career, ambivalent about her boyfriend, always short of money. Would she change places with her sister? In a minute. Except for the fear that staying home with children all day would turn her into an obese alcoholic who had affairs with the delivery-men.

What about working motherhood? It sounded good in the magazines, but Nina couldn't banish the image of Ida, when the kids were young, being so tired all of the time. And the thought of hiring a housekeeper terrified her. Whenever anyone came into her home to perform a service she hid in the bedroom until they were gone. How would she arrange for someone to take care of her children if she was going to hide in the bedroom?

Besides, who was going to be the father of these children? Grant? Did that mean they would be little Lutherans who talked about leftist politics all the time? She just couldn't see it. And what would they do about money? Their combined salaries could barely pay for Pampers, much less nursery school tuition.

Nina considered the possibility that she wouldn't be

happy no matter what she did. That her chronic sense of dissatisfaction would always be with her. When she looked back on her life she couldn't come up with even one minute when she felt truly contented. As a kid, she'd escape from the Bronx on the IRT to walk around Central Park pretending that she was a privileged Dalton student who had just wandered over from her apartment on Park or Fifth. Or she'd head downtown to the Village and pretend that she was the child of a divorced sculptress. Later as an undergraduate in the New York State university system, she would wish she was someplace in New England, someplace more intellectual and more expensive. In law school she wanted to be at Yale Drama or studying writing in Iowa. Or anywhere else. Now, day after day in her office with the bars on the windows, she wished for carpeting, art on the walls, and someone with a British accent to screen her calls.

Was it direction she was begging for? Would that cure this constant gnawing dissatisfaction? Judah Lev didn't have to judge for himself whether or not his life was satisfactory. He left that to God. So what was he doing shoving his tongue down the throat of a thirty-five-year-old pagan? Something was wrong, Nina thought. He might be in need of a little direction himself.

20

NINA HAD THEATER TICKETS with her friend Linda. She only went to the theater with friends. Grant was too cheap to go to the theater, and Ida had seen everything for half price by the time Nina even got around to thinking about it. Her mother shopped for culture the way other women shopped for fashion.

Nina was a woman with friends. Too many, in fact. She had spent her adulthood overcompensating for a lonely childhood. She couldn't stem the impulse to cultivate everyone she met who displayed the tiniest bit of intelligence or sensitivity. When she finally acknowledged how overextended she was, it was too late. They called her at the office, they called her at home. They dropped by, they bought her theater tickets. She couldn't keep up with them. Especially the single ones.

Their singleness seemed to provide them with a source of never-ending energy. They went to the movies, the ballet, the opera, and the theater. They took courses, exercised, and traveled. Linda, for example, took tap dancing twice a week. Not to meet men, of course. The only men in the class were gay or Japanese. Apparently tap dancing was big in Japan. She tap-danced when she wasn't at her regular gym or at Richard Brown's film course at the New School, watching new releases at ten o'clock on a Sunday morning. Or exploring her past life regressions at the Open Center or taking some variation of sushi-making at the Learning Annex. All this after ten-hour days at the office. Nevertheless, Linda never fell asleep during the second act, not even during the week.

Lately Nina had been falling asleep a lot. It was getting embarrassing. It wasn't so bad if someone had gotten you a cheap ticket with a TDF voucher or something. Sleeping through a ten-dollar play wasn't much worse than sleeping through a seven-dollar movie, which she did guiltlessly. Sometimes two hours of peace and quiet were worth seven bucks. But when she had paid full price at the theater and slept through the entire second act, well, she just couldn't justify that expensive a nap. The truth was that she had gotten rather fond of television in the past few years. Of course it stunk, but she was fond of it anyway. Why spend thirty-five bucks to fall asleep at the theater when she could fall asleep during "L.A. Law" for free? Nina's friends, the culture vultures, were horrified. Why couldn't she at least watch public television? Because, Nina told them, Channel 13 put her to sleep faster than any other medium.

Lately she had been hit with the uncontrollable urge to stay home. Being with Grant made it easy. Instead of planning an interesting excursion every weekend, she could just hang around and order in Chinese food. And blame it on him. He was cheap. He was a lump. He was a couch potato. Nobody suspected that she was just as bad. If she left him, she'd have to be out there doing exciting things. The thought was exhausting, not to mention expensive.

Was she starting to resemble Leo Fischman, whose idea of a vacation had been a double feature at the Loews Paradise? Middle age crept in on little cat's feet. She comforted herself with the idea that it was only a phase. When she got old, she'd have more energy again. Look at Ida. Her seventy-year-old mother could go one-on-one with any of Nina's friends and beat them easily.

That night as she fought to stay awake at the theater, she went over the evening's dinner conversation. Linda had put forth her requirements when it came to dating. She wouldn't go out with anyone who didn't like opera, who wasn't in good physical shape, or who made less money than she did. Dating didn't seem to be something Nina wanted to do. It was like being a one-woman draft board that had to check hundreds of men for potential defects.

Nina finally succumbed to sleep but managed to rouse herself in time to applaud enthusiastically at the curtain. She had liked the play. The fact that she had fallen asleep didn't mean anything. She had fallen asleep at some of her favorite plays. As the audience trooped excruciatingly slowly toward the exit sign, Nina and Linda man-watched. The theater was a great place for this, since it was one of the few New York City locations open to the public where you could get a good-sized crowd composed of people who uniformly looked as if they had stepped out of a Peugeot ad.

"Look at the eyes on that one." Linda pointed to a man in a Burberry on the landing below them. Nina managed to make eye contact with him. His eyes were startlingly blue. It took her a few seconds to realize that they belonged to West Estate's housing court counsel. He looked at Nina with mild confusion. Recognition dawned on him slowly.

Nina smiled and waved and tried to catch up with him, but the staircase was too jammed. He leaned over and whispered something to the woman at his side, a blond Peugeot type. She nodded and the couple picked their way through the crowd in the lobby. Nina tried to do the same, but by the time she reached the street they were gone. Their sudden disappearance was suspicious, since there were no cabs to be had.

While Nina stood in the street, looking east and west, Linda joined her. "I said look at his eyes, not chase him out of the theater. Why did you run after him like that?"

Nina recounted the episode in housing court. "Next time I'm in court, I'll stop at the clerk's office and take a look at the papers. Find out where he works. Maybe he'll grant me an audience and shed some light on the whole thing."

"Find out where he works and then find out if he's married," Linda said.

Nina looked at Linda. Despite all the tap dancing and self-improvement, she was still chubby and slightly disheveled and had a pronounced New York accent. Why did these women continue to hold on to their Robert Redford fantasies? They should never have made that movie, *The Way We Were*. It had done untold damage.

21

DANIELLE'S BIRTHDAY PARTY WAS a smash. The weather was perfect, the clown was funny, and the cake was excellent. Nina tried to watch two dozen adorable four-year-olds without feeling sorry for herself. It wasn't quite possible. She and Ida hung around for some post-party gossip.

"How many Rachels were there?" Nina asked her niece.

"Two," said Danielle.

"Rebecca seems to be taking over from Rachel and Sarah, the way Daniel started to take over from Benjamin," Nina said to Laura.

"What's on the horizon?" asked Laura.

"Why? Are you in need of another baby name by any chance?"

"Just curious."

"For girls I see Leah as next year's dark horse. For boys I see Daniel maintaining the lead."

"How did you get to be an expert?" asked Ken.

"I watch trends. If you can't set them, you might as well watch them," said Nina.

"Sarah," said Danielle. "There are more Sarahs than anything. In my class, there's big Sarah, little Sarah, and red Sarah."

"Is red Sarah a revolutionary?" asked Nina.

Danielle looked doubtful. "I don't know. But she does have red hair."

Nina pictured a little redheaded girl in guerrilla garb. It reminded her of a story that someone had told her years ago. Grandma had flown out to Berkeley to visit. The family was sitting at the dinner table. The little kid had been trained for the week preceding Grandma's visit to say "May I please be excused?" before she left the table. Halfway through the meal the kid stood up. Her grandmother's chair was blocking her escape. "Grandma," she said, "may I please be excused?" "But you haven't finished your dinner, dear," said Grandma. "May I please be excused?" the kid said again, politely. "Finish your dinner first." "May I please be excused?" she repeated, impatiently this time. "Not until you finish your dinner," Grandma replied firmly. The little kid finally looked Grandma straight in the eye and said "Move, motherfucker."

She supposed those days were gone. Now an epithet like "red Sarah" would be used for a girl who had red hair, or it could just as easily mean a four-year-old who favored red leather accessories. Last winter Nina had seen a toddler on Columbus Avenue in a fur coat. She had known for a while that it was only a matter of time, but when she finally saw her, it came as a shock anyway.

"How's the murder investigation progressing?" asked Ken.

Nina and Ida brought everyone up to date.

"It's just so spooky," Laura said. "I get this image of little old ladies all up and down West End Avenue dropping like flies."

"I know," said Ida. "I just hope I'm not next."

"I think it's sad, Mrs. Gross dying during Passover," said Nina. "There she is, saying 'Next year in Jerusalem,' and suddenly there is no next year."

"She must have been eating poison matzohs," said Danielle.

Everyone laughed. Ida said, "Yeah, I better stay out of that half-empty box of matzoh meal that Mrs. Gross's daughter foisted on me after her mother died."

Five seconds elapsed while Ida and Nina stared at each other with their mouths open. Finally Ida spoke. "Oh, my God. The groceries. I completely forgot. I have a cabinet filled with Mrs. Gross's leftover groceries. I wonder how high their digitalis content is.

"I can't believe we forgot about the groceries," said Nina. "What exactly do you have in your kitchen?"

"Everything. I have her flour, sugar, salt, matzoh meal. All her staples.Don't you remember? I showed them to you that day we were eating her macaroons."

"You're lucky you're both alive," said Laura.

"The macaroons were in an unopened tin," Nina explained. "But I bet it's the matzoh meal. Since she died during Passover, the matzoh meal becomes highly suspicious."

"You're overlooking something," said Ida.

"What's that?"

"Old ladies don't use their flour or sugar or salt. Sure, they might use their flour and sugar to bake sometimes, but what with diabetes and all, they rarely eat what they bake. They force it on their grandchildren and neighbors. And they also stay away from salt. Hypertension and all that. Especially Mrs. Gross. She was a real health nut. But come the holidays, I'm sure she couldn't resist making a little matzoh ball soup, for tradition's sake."

"So you think everything has digitalis in it?" asked Nina.

"Definitely. But it wasn't until Pesach came and she dipped into the matzoh meal that she got a sufficient dose to knock her off."

"And the digitalis in the cockroach powder was probably just spillage from the stuff that was put into the food," said Nina.

"Right," said Ida.

"We've got to have the groceries tested immediately," said Nina. "I'll stop at your house tonight and take them into Judah Lev tomorrow."

Ida shook her head. "No, I'd rather Ken have his lab run the first series of tests. We'd have more control that way." She turned to her son-in-law. "Ken, you must arrange to have those tests run first thing tomorrow. Which means you have to drive us home and pick up the samples tonight."

"Are you kidding?" he whined. "The car is good until Tuesday. Do you know how hard it is to get a parking space in the Slope these days? These streets are becoming choked with Volvo station wagons."

"Ken, this is important," Ida said firmly.

"So hard," he continued, "that they're selling spots in a garage condominium over on Union Street for thirty-two grand. And they're almost sold out. Actually they went on the market for twenty-nine thousand and I thought they were crazy. Who ever thought that they'd appreciate three grand in two months? The only downside is that even if you can get financing, considering the new tax laws, you can't deduct the interest on the mortgage."

"Shut up and drive," Ida said. "I'll pay for a parking lot if you can't find a space when you get home."

"I can't believe it," Nina said. "My brother-in-law the doctor with the Central Park West practice. And he's still playing alternate-side-of-the-street parking."

Ken gave Nina the finger. But he went to retrieve his car keys, and forty-eight hours later Ida and Nina found out what they wanted to know—all of the open boxes of groceries contained generous amounts of digitalis. The powder used to exterminate roaches was also present.

Judah Lev told Nina to bring the samples to his office right away. Her excitement mounted as she sat on the subway in her suit with her briefcase and two shopping bags full of groceries. She thought she made an odd picture, but New Yorkers being who they were, no one even shot her a glance. By the time she got to his office, she was practically jumping up and down. She had that heart-pounding breathless feeling that she got during closing arguments in court. But Judah Lev's response was less than wildly enthusiastic.

"It certainly doesn't hurt our case," he said as he traced the Hebrew lettering on the matzoh meal box with his finger.

"Jesus Christ," said Nina, "you're so impossibly judicious. Can't you be a little more enthusiastic? We've just come up with a piece of evidence that provides the only missing link in an otherwise clear-cut murder. I thought you'd be thrilled."

"I'm sorry you don't appreciate my judiciousness. I always thought of it as one of my better traits. Nina, you should keep in mind that it's a long road from this box of matzoh meal to a conviction."

Nina noted the way he said "a long road," with great satisfaction. It seemed to her that there were two kinds of people in the world, The kind who viewed the prospect of "a long road" as a challenge worth meeting. And the kind who viewed it as enough to make one throw oneself in front of a moving subway train. Judah was clearly the former. Nina was the latter. She had been that way for as long as she could remember. "Let's get it over with" had been her mantra since childhood. The other smart kids in her classes had taken great pride in turning in thoroughly researched, carefully written homework. They had an extensive collection of colored pencils that they kept carefully sharpened. Nina had only leaky Bic pens or chewed pencil stubs and had never used a loose-leaf reinforcement in her life. Her notebook looked like something a shopping bag lady would schlepp around the city with her.

The colored-pencil brigade had followed Nina through

life. They had shown up at Bronx Science with lab books containing carefully plotted multicolor bar and line graphs. In college they had owned both pink and yellow highlighters, whose use depended on how much emphasis the sentence demanded. You could always tell which texts belonged to Nina. The first chapter would be filled with illegible notes scribbled in the margins. The following chapters remained unread. Law school was even worse, of course. There they would arrive in class with typewritten case briefs, the holding printed in caps at the top of the first page. These days they were still around, all over her office, their case files neat and complete and a chrono file of their correspondence in its own folder. And here was Judah Lev, yet another member of the colored-pencil brigade.

"We have several obstacles," he said. "First of all, even though it has become clear that Mrs. Gross was poisoned, it's difficult to prove that it was the exterminator who poisoned her. Someone else could have put the digitalis in the groceries and spilled some into the cockroach powder in the process."

"That's ridiculous," Nina said. "There can be only one reason for West Estates going to all the trouble of hiring their own exterminator, and that was to poison Mrs. Gross. Nothing else makes sense."

"It's too much of a leap for a jury to make. I can't bring a case to trial based on that kind of reasoning. But—I do have another piece of evidence that points to the guilt of West Estates, not that it does me much good at this moment."

"What's that?"

"Myron Kaplan has disappeared. And we still don't know who the principals of West Estates are."

"How can a lawyer just disappear?" Nina said. "I mean a lawyer with an office and a secretary and a practice and everything?"

"He disappears the same way anyone else disappears. He

closes up shop and leaves. I don't think he had much of a practice, by the way, although he did in the past. These days, West Estates seems to be his main client. There was a bit of a scandal a couple of years ago. He was censured by the bar for getting a little too intimate with a client's escrow fund—I think that put a damper on his practice."

"How did he get wind of your investigation?"

"Maybe the investigator I sent over had something to do with it," he said mournfully. "Now I'm going to have to comb through piles of documents to see if I can get some idea of who, if anyone, was behind Kaplan."

Nina sighed. Maybe her office was the only place for her to practice law. There everything was over almost before it started. You got a client on intake day, rushed down to housing court the next day, screamed at the landlord, pleaded with the judge, negotiated with opposing counsel in the hallway, and before you knew it, both your client and the landlord were signing a handwritten stipulation. And that was it. Brief transactions, that's what Nina liked. If she had written *No Exit* her idea of hell would have been the IBM antitrust case where hundreds of lawyers pored over mile-high stacks of documents for years. And here was Judah Lev making her exciting little murder sound like just so much drudgery. She decided to try making a pass at him to shut him up.

"Not in the office," he said, planting her firmly back in her chair on the other side of his desk. "It's unprofessional."

There was that word. It set her off even more than "a long road" did. In this decade it seemed that everyone was judging everything on that basis. Purple patent leather shoes that she thought were adorable were suddenly "unprofessional." So was using Yiddish during negotiations. And the Gustav Klimt nude that had hung in her office since the day she started working had to come down for the same reason. When had people started using this dangerous and despicable word? It had slipped into the vernacular unnoticed, taken root, and had spread like a weed, threatening to choke all of her favorite flowering plants. She thought back to college, remembering an off-campus party where everyone had been tripping. Someone had dressed a dog in a tie-dyed shirt. The Jefferson Airplane blasted so loud it hurt. People sat on the floor staring alternately at the dog and at a Day-Glo poster on the ceiling. What if she had gotten up at that party and announced that by the time they were thirty-five they'd be telling each other that walking around the office with your suit jacket off was unprofessional. Everyone would have assumed she was having a bad trip. Lillian Hellman had been prescient when she said, during the McCarthy period, looking at all the cute little baby boomers in their Davy Crockett hats, that this generation was going to be the worst ever.

Nina never used the word. Well, she actually had told her sister on a few occasions, while flipping through the dress racks at Loehmann's, that she simply couldn't wear this or that to the office because it was you-know-what. And she had to admit that she used it with a bit of contempt for her sister, who didn't have a profession. That was the problem with that word. It was horribly contemptuous.

Judah Lev was describing the documents he had to search through in order to discover the true identity of the principals of West Estates. He'd contacted Albany for their designation of the secretary of state for service of process. And he'd contacted the state attorney general's office to see if they had a broker-dealer statement on file. Neither agency had yet responded. Nina's mind wandered.

It seemed that a murder really had been committed, Nina thought. Two murders, in fact. Somehow she still didn't believe it. She had set off on this investigative path with Ida because it seemed like a fun adventure. But she had never really expected to uncover anything. Nothing this extraordinary had ever happened to her before. Of course she had her share of adventures, sometimes with surprising and amusing results. Like having a quasi-affair with an Orthodox Jewish prosecutor. But this murder stuff was in another league. It was the kind of thing that changed your life. She monitored herself. Let's see, do I feel as if my life has been changed? Nina emptied her mind to see what thoughts would fill it up. The usual ones came flooding back. Should she break up with Grant? Should she change careers? Were the strawberries in her refrigerator rotten yet? Nah, she thought, same old shit. What would it take, then, to change her life? To turn her into a focused, unambivalent, contented person? Maybe cancer. She had read articles about people having successfully battled cancer and no longer agonizing about the meaning of their existence. Maybe cancer would do that for her.

Judah Lev interrupted her thoughts. "Nina, I get the feeling that you're not paying attention. What are you thinking about?"

"Nothing," she said.

"Somehow I find that hard to believe."

Should she tell him that she was thinking about cancer? Bad idea. He might think of her as depressingly meshuga as opposed to charmingly meshuga. "Sex," she said, trying to be upbeat. "Come to dinner at my house tomorrow night."

"Your kitchen isn't kosher. I won't be able to eat anything."

"I'm sure we'll find something for you to eat." She batted her eyelashes in mock seduction.

22

NINA SURVEYED HER TABLETOP. As a seduction scene, it left a lot to be desired. She had tried to do everything tastefully—flowers, tablecloth, candles, kosher champagne in an ice bucket. But the paper plates and plastic forks somehow detracted. This kosher stuff was a pain. She had cooked everything in disposable Broil-a-Foil. Judah Lev had okayed her salad bowl, since it was used for uncooked food only. She considered telling him about warm salad with prosciutto, but decided to keep her mouth shut. The salad bowl was the only decent-looking piece on the table. How did people live like this? Life was complicated enough, what with subway delays and insurance forms. Why add to it?

She knew that most kosher people found their own ways to cope with the restrictions. Like her friend Linda and her air cheeseburgers. Linda had grown up in a kosher home. As kids, she and her brother would make air cheeseburgers to get around their mother's dietary code. Since a cheeseburger, with its mixture of meat and milk, is inherently tref, it couldn't be allowed to come into contact with a dish or pan. Anything tref could permanently alter the utensil's kosher status. But the kids had fallen in love with cheeseburgers. So they'd cook the hamburger part in a meat pan and broil the cheese on a bun in the oven (the toaster oven had yet to be invented) and put them together in the air. They'd eat the cheeseburger standing up so it wouldn't touch the table.

Nina felt as if she were making air cheeseburgers. The whole thing seemed a farce to her. But Judah Lev must have known, when he consented to come for dinner, that one layer beneath the Broil-a-Foil was a surface that had touched all kinds of strange and forbidden foods. So had her mouth, for that matter, and she hadn't noticed him displaying any hesitancy about coming into contact with that. Tonight would reveal how he felt about coming into contact with the rest of her.

And how did she feel about coming into contact with the rest of him? Why was she having this seduction dinner anyway? She had been getting a kick out of their innocent affair. It was fun to make out passionately in the back of a taxi and then tear yourself apart at the curb. It was very romantic, actually. She felt like a character in a forties movie, who drank manhattans and met men under the clock at the Biltmore. Last week she had bought a pair of seamed stockings. So why push this forward? After all, if it was the sex act she was after, there was always Grant. Even though the passion was not what it had been in the beginning, Grant knew how to make her come. That was the good thing about long-term relationships: they resulted in orgasms. So why was it that the most memorable and exciting nights had all been spent with new men who hadn't even gotten her close? She often felt that she could live without orgasms. The only time she didn't feel that way was right after she had had one.

She couldn't exactly figure out her motives for having Judah Lev to dinner. It just seemed like the natural progression of things. She couldn't imagine what it would be like to continue this kiss-him-goodnight dating business. Her generation wasn't particularly good at dating. They had gotten a late start. It didn't seem to be much fun, no matter how old you were. The media covered the dating scene much the way they had covered Vietnam. A reporter would go to a bar or a dance and interview the casualties as if it were My Lai. Nina's friends talked about dating the way they talked about dieting. Dating was good for you. If you didn't watch yourself you'd slip into celibacy. "Go out there and date," they told one another. "First thing Monday morning, buy a copy of *New York* magazine and read the personals."

Her relationship with Grant had exempted Nina from most of this. Although she felt that she should be finding a husband, which Grant didn't seem to be. So she read the personals every week, just to see. They were fascinating, although she hated all that slim, trim, model-class-looks crap. She had never answered one, but was constantly drafting her own. Only in her head, of course. She had yet to set anything down on paper. Lately her mental drafts kept drifting in very traditional directions, no matter how hard she tried to pull them back. Her ideal man was starting to bear an alarming similarity to her brother-in-law. She had even thought of a good lead. "Let me be your parasite," it would begin.

Judah Lev would make a good husband. For someone else. She didn't think she wanted to convert. Although all that structure seemed appealing compared to the chaos that was her life. But she didn't want to cover her head with a shaytl. Her hair was her best feature. And having to wear a long-sleeved dress all summer would be awful. Those women must have enormous dry-cleaning bills. Well, if Judah Lev wasn't a husband and wasn't a lover, what was he? He was a good kisser, was all she could say.

What should she wear for this intimate dinner? She had a black silk nightgown for special sexual occasions, but that seemed wrong. She could just imagine him walking in and telling her she looked unprofessional. She settled for black pants and a jersey that showed a lot of collarbone.

It was already after eight, his scheduled arrival time. She used to time the vinaigrette to coincide with the moment a man walked in. It seemed romantic to be whisking at his first sight of her. Now it seemed contrived. Let him find her as she really was. Slumped on the couch watching sitcom reruns. But once the intercom buzzed, she quickly shut off the set. Watching reruns was like masturbating or nose-picking. Something you could only do when no one else was there.

Judah Lev arrived with a strangely shaped bundle under his arm. It clearly wasn't champagne or flowers. It turned out to be a variety of items from the appetizer counter, just in case her attempts at kosher cuisine didn't live up to his strict rabbinical standards.

Nina was dismayed. "That's the story of my life," she said. "I plan a quiet seduction dinner and the object of my affections brings appetizers."

"Is that what this is? A seduction dinner?" Judah Lev looked pleased.

"It was supposed to be. Until you showed up with whitefish." She turned to whip up the vinaigrette. Maybe in the Orthodox community a whisk was still considered an erotic utensil. Conveniently, her kitchen counter was in the same room as her couch.

"Don't let my whitefish spoil your plans." He crossed the room and wrapped his arms around her from behind. His nose nudged her ear as he gently rubbed both breasts. She stood still, letting him go on and on. She could spend days like this. There was nothing more pleasurable than a really good breast massage. Finally she turned and they fell onto the couch. One of those wonderful scenes unfolded where pieces of clothing are slowly removed, one by one, with a lot of great stuff in between.

Countless orgasms later, Judah Lev's tongue was still going strong. It had the skill and knowledge that she thought only her own hand could possess. Finally he took a breather. Anxious to return the favor, her mouth traveled down to his very erect penis.

"Nina, don't." He reached for his shorts.

"Why not?" She leaned back and covered her breasts with a couch pillow.

"Look, it's like being kosher," he explained. "People write their own rules. Some people will eat this, but not that. Other people will eat that, but not this."

"You can eat me, but I can't eat you, is that it?"

"I don't spill my seed." It was comical to hear such a biblical pronouncement from a naked man sitting on her couch with a huge erection.

"Well, what do you do with your seed, if you don't spill it? You appear to have collected quite a bit of seed there."

"I think it's time for dinner." He slipped on his pants, sat down at the table, and dived into the food. He consumed course after course, displaying no concern over the kosher status of any of it. Nina watched his crotch as he ate. The bulge only seemed to get bigger as he worked his way through the meal. It was still there when he kissed her good night and left.

What was that all about? Nina wondered as she cleaned up the remains of dinner. It seemed so improbable. Judah Lev sitting there with a huge erection, proclaiming, "I don't spill my seed." He was supposed to be a force of stability in her life. To teach her a lesson about taking herself seriously, about respecting institutions, about calming down. Jesus, he was just as crazy as she was. This always happened. Nina would go out with some CEO type, hoping he would instill in her a healthy reverence for capitalism, pushing her further along the road to riches. And the guy would end up whining all night about how he really wanted to live in a cabin in the Adirondacks and write a novel. Or she would befriend a nice young woman who seemed contentedly married, hoping to get an inside glimpse of marriage as a successful institution. And before she knew it, the woman would be confessing to a long-standing affair with her child's math tutor. Was it that she attracted these types? Or was it that everyone was discontentedly insane? It was unsettling to think that the latter was true. Especially when it came to politicians. She pictured George Bush dressing up in his wife's underwear and William Rehnquist jerking off to a videocassette of "Debbie Does Dallas." It made her nervous.

If everyone was crazy, maybe she should just go ahead and marry Grant. It was true that his eccentric tendencies drove her nuts, but at least they were benign tendencies. The tendency to believe that housing court was the center of the universe. To order orange juice as a before-dinner drink. To refuse to pay seven dollars to see a movie. Actually that tendency was becoming less than benign, since it excluded virtually all Manhattan movies these days. The only time they got to see anything unrevived was when they visited Terry and Steve in the country.

Yet there were far worse eccentric tendencies in the world. She heard horror stories all the time. The tendency to carry on covert homosexual affairs for decades and not tell your wife until your lover was diagnosed as having AIDS. The tendency to sell your family's home to pay your gambling debts. And now here was the tendency to not spill your seed. Well, that was unfair of her. She was sure that once Judah Lev was married to some nice observant young woman, he'd spill his seed plenty. Enough to make so many little Levs that he'd need a time share in the maternity ward at Mount Sinai.

23

OH, SHIT, THOUGHT NINA, as her new client handed her a document. I know what this is going to be.

Even though the paper was folded into a small package, Nina could tell it was a seventy-two-hour notice. Not a regular dispossess where she could leisurely schedule a court date the next time she was downtown. A seventy-two-hour notice meant you had to drop everything and run to court before the marshal arrived to throw your client's possessions down the stairs. "When did you get this, Mrs. Santorini?"

"They taped it to my door on Monday."

It was Wednesday. There went Nina's afternoon. If she didn't go down there today, it would be too late. "Okay, Mrs. Santorini, tell me the whole story." She sat back to listen.

It was a mournful narrative. "I've been living in this apartment for twenty-five years," the old lady said. Most of these sagas started similarly. Some of the elderly tenants had a history of landlord troubles. But many, like Mrs. Santorini, had lived for decades uninterrupted by disputes until recently, when their landlords decided the apartment would be worth more vacant than occupied. These decisions often coincided with a decision to turn the building into a co-op. Mrs. Santorini had been paying her rent on the tenth of the month for years, when all of a sudden she got hit with a hefty late penalty. She refused to pay it, so the landlord started returning her rent checks, then served her with a dispossess notice and added legal fees to the amount due. Instead of going to court, she had her daughter write him a letter, and now he had a warrant of eviction. Nina had heard this story from many old ladies. Some of the old ladies sobbed; some of them sputtered with indignant wrath. Mrs. Santorini seemed too stunned to display any emotion. That was a bad sign. It was this paralysis that had gotten her this close to eviction. Nina would have to shake her out of it. She'd shake her out of it tomorrow. Today she had better haul her ass down to court.

Nina brooded as she sat on the subway, her briefcase cradled between her feet. It was already two o'clock. She'd have to run to the clerk's office, get them to find the file, fill out the forms for an order to show cause, and wait around until the judge signed it. Then both the marshal and the landlord would have to be served before five o'clock today to prevent an eviction tomorrow. If she had any luck, one of her office investigators would be hanging around the court-house and would serve the order this afternoon. If not, she'd have to waste time tracking them down. Her mind ranged over the usual set of defenses. At this late stage in the game, she usually had to make an argument claiming defective service of the dispossess notice in order to have the case reopened. How many times had she done this, racked her brain on the subway for a defense that didn't sound trite and contrived? Walked down Franklin Street to the courthouse while the men loading bolts of fabric onto the trucks whistled and winked at her. Actually, over the years, as the fabric jobbers on Franklin Street were replaced by expensive residential lofts, there were fewer men. And the remaining ones whistled and winked at her less often than when she had first started walking down Franklin Street. Well, she was older now and less vulnerable. City women knew that it was your look of vulnerability, more than big tits or short skirts, that caused men to roll their eyes and moan "mamacita" at you. And Nina's vulnerability was getting pretty used up.

Assuming she found one of her investigators, it was still going to be too late to go back to the office after court. Maybe she would go to Syms and cruise the dress racks. The store would be filled with women lawyers on their way to and from court. The way the bar at Peggy Doyle's filled up with their brethren. There was something else she had to do next time she was in the clerk's office. It had been nagging at the back of her mind, but she couldn't quite remember what it was. She poked through the zippered compartment of her brief-case, where she threw all her miscellany. She came up with a bunch of cash-machine withdrawal receipts and an assort-ment of business cards from opposing counsel. And a scrap of paper with a court index number on it. She was always doing that, scribbling down phone numbers and index numbers with nothing further to identify them. What was this one? She stared at it. Suddenly she remembered. It was West Estates v. Singer, the case where that Wall Street-type had given her the brush-off in the hallway and later in the theater. She'd been meaning to look at that file for a while now. Today she'd definitely have time while she was waiting around for the judge to sign the order to show cause.

Nina raced down Franklin Street, hurried into the court-house, and headed straight for the motion part, just to see who was sitting that week. She was glad to see Sally Quinn at the bench. Sally was probably as good as you could get if you had to get an order signed. Too bad it was already Wednesday and too late to get a return date for this week. She'd prefer to argue this motion in front of her. Sally Quinn had come out of New York's first women's law collective to become a deputy commissioner at Housing Preservation and Development. It was a quick route to the bench. She was only a year or two older than Nina. Nina remembered the first time she'd noticed all of a sudden that fashion models and baseball players were no older than she was. Now it was retiring baseball players and judges. Soon it would be the president of the United States.

Sally Quinn gave her a brief wave, and then Nina ran off to the clerk's office. Nina got on line behind a pair of *pro se* tenants who were having a hard time filling out their forms. What the hell, she thought, it would be quicker to help them than not. She finished up their forms for them.

"Are you a lawyer, miss?" asked the woman of the pair.

"Yes, but not for hire," she said. Some former legal services attorneys made a living by hanging around housing court and picking up clients. Their offices were barely more than an answering machine and a typing service. But they were the best. They ate, breathed, and lived housing court. You always knew where to find them and never even had to waste a quarter on a phone call. It didn't appeal to Nina, though, as a career move. They reminded her of those albino alligators that supposedly lived in the New York sewer system and had never seen the light of day.

Nina filled out her file request form and the clerk brought Mrs. Santorini's file over. The landlord's papers were enough of a mess to make proper service a viable issue. She'd ask for a traverse hearing on service next week on her return date when she made her motion. For now she simply listed defective service along with breach of warranty of habitability. She handed them back to the clerk. "About how long would you say?" she asked him.

"Quinn's calendar is pretty backed up today," he said. "You're going to be here for a while."

"That's okay. I've got plenty to keep me busy." Nina did a quick search of the hall for a familiar face. She got lucky. One of her staff investigators was hanging around the hallway. He promised to stay put until she got her order signed. Then she went back to the clerk's office. "Could you do me a favor?" she said. "This isn't one of mine, but I need to take a look at it." She filled out a request form with the index number of West Estates v. Singer.

"Sure thing." He fetched the file for her.

Nina examined the file. The papers looked like a set for any other holdover proceeding, but they yielded some interesting information. Mrs. Singer's apartment was on West End Avenue, as the lawyer had said, a few blocks up from Ida's. Apparently the case had been withdrawn. The unusual thing about this file was the petitioner's attorney: Case & Clark, a big white-shoe law firm, was handling this proceeding. Usually evictions were handled by landlord mills. It was true that sometimes a big firm would handle an eviction for one of their corporate clients as a favor. Perhaps West Estates was a substantial client of Case & Clark in other matters. But what, in that case, were they doing with a schlepper like Myron Kaplan? It didn't make any sense.

She took another look at the papers. The dotted line for the petitioner's signature contained an illegible scrawl. Deciphering it wouldn't help anyway. The petitioner's attorney was permitted to execute the dispossess notice, and this was probably the signature of someone at Case & Clark. She could try to pry some information out of someone at the law firm, but it was probably pointless. Attorneys were under no obligation to give out information about their cases to nosy members of the public, and she saw no reason why they would in this case. Even if Judah Lev subpoenaed the case file, they could always invoke the attorney-client privilege. She handed the file back reluctantly. She would have to look elsewhere for a lead.

As she waited for the judge to clear her calendar, she settled down with the *Times*. She was deep into the Living section, wondering whether she should try making eggplant jam, when the clerk called her into the courtroom. Sally Quinn beckoned her up to the bench.

"Your Honor," Nina began, "this is a non-payment case where there are serious issues of improper service."

"Pick a return date," said Quinn, as she smiled and signed the order.

"A week from today would be fine."

"Good enough."

"I wish all my oral arguments were that persuasive."

"Everyone gets their day in court," said the judge. "You've had more than your share, haven't you? How many years has it been?"

"I'm still in the single digits, thank you very much."

"Ever think about leaving legal services? Going out on your own or into government?"

"Sure, I think about it. And I think about living in a cabin in Montana or in a cave in Greece. I think about it all the time. I just don't do anything about it."

"The cave in Greece. Now, that sounds good. Let me know if you want company. Not this week, though. My calendar's all backed up."

"Don't worry, Your Honor. I don't think it'll be this week."

"Keep in touch," Sally Quinn said, as she turned back to her docket.

"Thanks for the order to show cause."

"Any time."

Nina raced out of the courtroom to find her investigator. It was almost four, which would barely give him time to serve the landlord and the marshal. But would give her plenty of time to go to Syms. Or to the Union Square greenmarket on her way home to pick up some eggplants for the

Times recipe. But she really wasn't in an eggplant jam kind of mood. And she was too far along in her menstrual cycle to venture trying on anything that had a waist. She ended up going back to the office because that was what she did for a living.

24

"**Y**OUR FRIEND PAID US a visit," Ida said.

"What friend?" asked Nina.

"Judah Lev."

"Who's us?"

"My co-op." Ida and Nina were sitting at Ida's dining room table, trying not to eat. "He interviewed our managing agent."

"I'm glad to hear he's earning his paycheck. What did he want to know?" Nina was miffed with him. He hadn't turned up any new leads. He also hadn't asked her out since her dinner party. What good was he?

"He wanted to trace the latest maintenance check we received from West Estates."

"And what did he find out? Or don't you know?"

"Of course I know," said Ida indignantly. "The name of the account is West Estates Special Two. Not very revealing, is it? It's a non-interest-bearing checking account in one of the big local commercial banks, and the maintenance was paid by electronic transfer."

"What's electronic transfer? Sounds like a rock group."

"It means that instead of actually cutting a check and putting it in an envelope, you access your account by computer and transfer the funds to the payee electronically."

"Which means no postmark, no cover letter, no indication of who's paying or where he's paying from. Right?" said Nina.

"Right. Except I assume that the bank has a record of where the transfer was made."

"So somewhere out there, someone with a hard disk is keeping the account current, but only the bank knows his identity."

"I suppose so," said Ida. "I assume Judah Lev has contacted the bank, but I don't know what he's come up with. I got as much as I could out of the managing agent. You haven't heard anything, have you?"

"No, he's been sort of incommunicado lately."

"I see." Ida didn't push it.

"I did finally find the court file on that Singer woman I told you about. It didn't reveal much. Only that some big Wall Street law firm was representing West Estates in court. But it didn't give a clue as to who the principals are. What we need to find out is the names of the individual shareholders and officers of the corporation."

"The individual shareholders," Ida said thoughtfully. "Hmm, that gives me an idea. I hadn't thought of it before. The shares allocated to Mrs. Gross's apartment should be held by an individual."

"I thought they were held by West Estates as a corporate entity."

"Originally they were. But think back."

"Back to when?" Nina wasn't following her mother.

"Back to the days before the Tax Reform Act of 1986."

"Well, it wasn't exactly a landmark in my life," said Nina. After all these years she was still filing the short form.

"The Internal Revenue Service used to require holders of unsold shares in co-ops to designate individuals as shareholders after three years."

"That sounds pretty obscure. How do you know this?"

"Only because it was something the board was vigilant about. It used to be that failure to designate an individual could jeopardize the tax deductions of all the shareholders in the co-op. We'd all be unable to deduct our mortgage interest and real-estate taxes."

"But these weren't unsold shares. Rabinowitz, the landlord, sold them to West Estates, didn't he?"

"Yes, technically," said Ida. "But according to our bylaws, the shares remain unsold until they're purchased for occupancy. That's not uncommon. You understand?"

"Yeah, I see." Nina was always amazed to see how the purchase of an apartment seemed to turn even the most unsophisticated business mind into a tax genius. Her mother used to be the kind of woman who would shrug and say she didn't know from such things.

"Now, let's see. West Estates bought that apartment soon after the conversion. It would be around 1982, I think. Three years later would be '85. Which predates the 1986 tax act. So they must have designated an individual to hold those shares in 1985."

"Would the board have a record of that?" Nina finally gave in and opened the refrigerator.

"Absolutely." Ida followed her daughter into the kitchen. "Every time the shares are transferred, the secretary and the president of the board of directors have to reissue the shares in the name of the new holder. And the secretary has to execute a new proprietary lease. Then the secretary enters the transaction into the corporate ledger book."

Nina considered whether it was worth the trouble of toasting an English muffin. Probably not. There was nothing to put on it except Weight Watchers margarine. She closed the refrigerator. "Then we should check the records, right? Are they kept in the building?"

"Downstairs in the boardroom. The managing agent uses it as a part-time office."

"Can we get in there?"

"No problem." Ida went off to the bedroom to fetch her purse. She came back with an overloaded key chain.

"My God, look at all those keys. Are you moonlighting as a night watchman somewhere?"

Ida enumerated. "Three locks on my door, two locks on the lobby door just in case the doorman is off duty, the board-room, the boardroom file cabinet, my own file cabinet, your apartment, Laura's house in the city, Laura's house in the country, and my gym locker."

Nina always laughed at the thought of her mother at the gym. But many of Ida's friends were members. The old ladies were big on aquatics, which was aerobics in the water where their weight didn't work against them.

"Can we go down there now?" Nina checked her watch. "It's almost ten. Is it too late to be poking around there?"

"The later the better. We don't need to advertise this."

Nina and Ida remained silent as they slipped into the boardroom. The room was sparsely furnished. Bo Marsh's attempts to decorate it had been resisted to date. The board's one concession had been to permit him to paint the walls a pale lilac.

Ida unlocked the bottom drawer of the horizontal file cabinet. "Everything's filed by apartment," she said, as she flipped through the files. "Let me just find the..." Ida drifted off.

"What's the matter?"

"Wait a minute. Here's six-E, six-F, six-G, six-H, seven-B, seven-C. I can't believe it. The file for seven-A is gone."

"Is there any reason why it should be missing? Do people borrow them like in a lending library?"

"Absolutely not. Let's check the ledger book. We're very careful about entering everything in there. If there was a transfer of shares, it would be in there." Ida pulled open the top drawer of the file cabinet and took out a large ledger book. She carefully scrutinized it for a few minutes. "There's nothing here for seven-A during 1983, '84, '85, or '86. The only entry is the original transfer to West Estates in '82. But look at this." She showed Nina the book. One of the entries had been carefully inked over with a fountain pen, rendering it illegible.

"Who could have done that?"

"No one has access to these files except the board. Even the managing agent doesn't have a key to the cabinet." Ida went back to the bottom drawer and examined each file carefully. "I can't believe the file's not there. There must be something screwy going on with one of the board members."

"Or maybe several of them. Who knows? You could be the only one in the dark. Or maybe you're even lying to me. Did you kill Mrs. Gross, Ma? Tell the truth. It would be the perfect crime, you know. No one would ever suspect the retired Jewish schoolteacher."

"I'm not capable of murder. I have too big a mouth."

"I believe you. Who else is on the board?"

"Let's discuss this upstairs. All of a sudden I have an urgent desire to get the hell out of here." Ida replaced the ledger book and locked the file cabinet. She peeked cautiously out the door to make sure the lobby was empty before they left the room.

"Now let's make a chart," Ida said, once they were back upstairs. "I have Magic Markers, and I think I have some oak tag somewhere." She rummaged around in her hall closet.

"Oak tag. That's a blast from the past. Whatever happened to it? Did it become obsolete?"

"No, schoolteachers became obsolete."

"What do you mean?"

"Well, how many schoolteachers do you know?"

"Plenty."

"Under the age of sixty."

"None."

"See what I mean? Your generation decided to go to law school instead. There's nothing wrong with that. I'm very glad that you can go to the bathroom whenever you feel like it without having to get someone to cover your class."

"So who's teaching?"

"People who didn't go away to college."

"I rarely think of myself as overprivileged."

"Everything's relative," said Ida, as she carefully ruled her oak tag into quarters and wrote the name of a board member on each quarter.

"By the way, have you been discussing the murder at board meetings?"

"No, I've kept my mouth shut."

"How come?"

"Instinct, I guess. Now, Bo Marsh seems to be our prime suspect. He's the secretary, so it would have been up to him to reissue the shares and execute the new proprietary lease when West Estates designated an individual to hold them. He must have known something about this." Ida wrote "issued shares" under his name and then the name of the investment banking firm he worked for.

"Next is Bob Carroll. He's the only one of the board members I actively dislike. Is that enough to make him a suspect?"

"What the hell, why not?"

"Okay." Ida wrote "awful" under his name and then the name of the law firm he worked for. Which happened to be Case & Clark.

Nina jumped up and down. "That's the firm that represents West Estates in housing court."

"Very suspicious," said Ida. "But is it conclusive?"

"Let's run through the rest of our suspects before we conclude anything."

"Okay." Ida picked up her Magic Marker again. "Then there's Mark Cohen. He works for a Japanese bank, but I can't remember the name of it."

"Well, that's definitely suspicious."

"How come?"

"Since West Estates incorporated in the Netherlands Antilles they're probably foreigners. So there could easily be a Japanese connection."

"Right." Ida wrote "Tokyo" under his name. "That leaves Mark Sadow. He's an architect who has his own firm. There's nothing particularly suspicious about him," she said as she wrote "Mark Sadow Associates" under his name. "But there's a feeling I get about him. Not that he's unlikable, like Bob Carroll. But he's...I don't know. Something." Ida sat with her Magic Marker poised. Finally she wrote "greedy" under his name.

"Ma, this is 1980s New York City we're talking about. It takes a lot to have greedy written under your name. Is he that bad?"

"It's masked, but it's there. Trust me."

"Okay, what do we do next?"

Ida shrugged. "We call them all into a room and have Hercule Poirot tell us which one did it."

25

JUDAH LEV WAS AS CLOSE to Hercule Poirot as they had. A beard instead of a mustache, an Ortho instead of a Belgian. He graciously granted them an audience, so they schlepped Ida's chart with them. He laughed when he saw it. "What's the matter?" he said. "Your daughter wouldn't give you a yellow legal pad?"

"I think best in oak tag," Ida said. "It's my medium."

Judah Lev glanced over the chart. He pointed to Bob Carroll's name. "Here's our man. The fact that he works for Case and Clark does seem to be more than a coincidence. And Ida thinks he's awful. That should be enough for a conviction." He gave them a sort of smirk that carried more than a hint of condescension. Nina began to feel uneasy. Maybe she should stay away from this guy. If there was one thing she couldn't tolerate it was condescension. "But wait," he continued. "Here's someone who's greedy. What does that mean?"

"He has a Ferrari," explained Ida.

"The man is interested in having nice things for his family. Does that make him greedy?" The condescension had shifted to defensiveness.

"It was just a thought," Ida said.

Nina butted in. "I have nothing against nice things, but it seems a little ridiculous to have a Ferrari in Manhattan where some garages won't even take them. Don't you think paying fifteen grand a year in insurance, parking, and repair bills is a bit stiff for something you only get to drive for a few hours on the weekend?"

Nina pondered the distinction between greed and priorities. Where did one end and the other begin? Maybe there was nothing inherently wrong with greed. Perhaps it was only the unbridled kind that got you into trouble. Was that what had been wrong with her family? Neither of her parents had a greedy gene. Having a family without greed was like having a depressed immune system; it left you vulnerable to all sorts of things. Maybe greed was actually a protective device. Well, in that case marrying Grant would never do. He was completely devoid of the trait. And her own greed was defective. It sputtered and sparked, but never kicked in. There was one problem with this genetic theory of greed, Nina thought. And that was Laura. Despite two parents who seemed completely devoid of a reach that was even half as long as their grasp, Laura seemed completely capable of getting everything she wanted. Maybe Nina's sister was a mutant.

"Owning a Ferrari," said Judah Lev, "even in Manhattan, is not enough to convict someone of murder."

"Then let's convict Bob Carroll," Nina said.

"Getting a little impatient, are we?" He turned to Ida. "Will you please tell Nina that patience is a virtue?"

Ida shook her head. "Sorry, wrong daughter."

"It's gotta be Carroll," Nina said. "The Case and Clark connection is more than a coincidence."

"Hold on. You're forgetting something," Judah Lev said in his best colored-pencil-brigade manner. "This isn't an isolated murder we're talking about. We've come up with at least one other probable victim and who knows how many others. Bob Carroll might be the tip of the iceberg."

"Or no tip at all," said Ida.

"No tip? What makes you say that?" asked Judah Lev.

"Because I know the guy. He's awful, but he wouldn't participate in a murder."

"I'm sure you have good instincts about these things. But I'm going to try to get ahold of his tax returns anyway, just to see if he's holding the seven-A shares in addition to his own."

"Wait a minute," said Ida. "The managing agent must have a computerized list of shareholders. Our monthly maintenance bills are issued by computer. Maybe the individual holding the shares is on the list."

"We checked that already to see if we could get another address for the corporation. The bills are still being sent to West Estates, care of Myron Kaplan's office."

"My God, this is terrible," said Ida. "What if we had a tax audit and had to prove that the unsold shares were being held by an individual? We wouldn't be able to."

"Is that worse than your neighbor being killed?" asked Nina.

"To most of the shareholders in the building it probably would be. I myself am in a lower tax bracket than most and can afford to dwell on trivialities such as who killed Mrs. Gross."

"What about the bank?" Nina asked Judah Lev. "Did you find out where the maintenance payments are being electronically transferred from?

"According to the bank, they're still coming from Myron Kaplan's office."

"But that's closed down, isn't it?"

"Yeah, but the bank doesn't know that."

"I don't understand," said Nina.

"You can take your computer and your modem and move them someplace else and the bank has no way of knowing."

"Those transfers are done over the phone lines, aren't they?" asked Ida.

"Right."

"Can the phone company trace the call?"

"It's almost impossible. A call has to be traced while it's being made. The bank receives so many transfers that it's difficult to isolate this transaction and put a trace on it."

"So what's our strategy?" asked Ida.,

"I like this Bob Carroll lead a lot," Judah Lev said. "It's the first encouraging piece of information we've received in a while. I'm going to follow up on it with the IRS."

"I'm glad you're enthusiastic," said Ida. "But you wouldn't mind if I made a few inquiries around the building, would you?"

"Try to be discreet. I don't want Carroll getting wind of something and covering his tracks."

"If it is Carroll." Ida smiled sweetly. "Which I doubt," she added with scorn.

26

"THERE'S SOMETHING I NEED to speak with you about before next week's board meeting." Ida was on the telephone with Bo Marsh. It was good etiquette among the board members to phone, not to just drop in on each other. As in the rest of middle-class Manhattan society, ringing a doorbell without phoning first was tantamount to walking around with your fly open. It was sloppy and vulgar.

"I'm just out of the shower," said Bo Marsh. "Can I call you right back?"

"Would it be all right if I dropped by for a few minutes?"

"Okay." He didn't say it with great reluctance, but with that tiny hint of resentment that everyone seemed to have these days at the slightest intrusion. Receiving guests was like having to work overtime. "Give me ten minutes to put on some clothes."

Ida waited a polite fifteen before she set out. Bo Marsh opened the door wearing sweats. Not regular sweats like the ones college kids wore, gray or navy with school emblems printed on them. And not sweats like the ones they wore in the suburbs, turquoise and studded with bugle beads. But sweats worthy of the most sophisticated of Manhattan homosexuals. A shade between black and charcoal, purchased no doubt from one of those cavernous SoHo emporiums that feature only a rack or two of the most tasteful of garments. A store that can boast no less than ten square feet of floor space per clothing item. He had a body worthy of the several hundred dollars his sweat suit must have cost. Even his bare feet seemed muscular and well formed.

"Decaf espresso?" he asked, as he ushered her in.

"If it's not too much trouble."

"No trouble. The machine's all warmed up."

Ida followed him into the kitchen and watched him pump the coffee into a small exquisite pewter cup lined with white porcelain. The kitchen was a knockout. Gray cabinets, black granite countertops, white ceramic tile floor. "I'm afraid I don't have too much else to offer you in the way of refreshment," he said. "The larder stays pretty empty during the week." Bo had explained his theory of dieting to Ida on previous occasions. He had fast days and feast days. They both agreed on how unhealthful it was, but Bo was flattered by Ida's vocal admiration of the results.

"Please, the espresso's enough of a treat."

"Let's go into the living room." It was another great room, totally black and white except for a series of cobalt sconces. He put her coffee down on an Eileen Gray cigarette table that sat between two black leather Grand Confort sofas. "Now, what are we talking about?" he asked.

"We're talking about flip taxes." A flip tax was a surcharge imposed on the seller of an apartment and generally used to build up the co-op's reserve fund. People who intended to sell their apartments hated flip taxes. Those who had no intention of selling favored them. Ida figured that whoever was on the verge of selling 7A would probably be opposed to implementing a building-wide flip tax.

"Flip taxes. An idea whose time has gone." Bo Marsh looked less than thrilled.

"Why do you say that?"

"Not out of self-interest. I've no intention of selling in the foreseeable future."

"Now, Bo, we all know you have grand visions of retiring to Rio."

"Of course I do. Don't you?"

"Rio? Not my speed," said Ida. "Maybe the south of France."

"Whatever. But I just put twenty-five grand into my kitchen and I'll never pull it out when I sell. I figure I've got to stay put for at least a decade to amortize the countertops alone."

"So why not a flip tax?"

"Because I think it'll damage the value of the apartments in a very severe way. And that would be unfair to all of us."

"In what way?"

"Look up and down West End Avenue. What do you see? Two miles of co-op buildings, all almost exactly alike. And Broadway is becoming a regular condoland. There must be five thousand newly constructed condominium units over there. There's just too much product in the neighborhood. I'm afraid the market could really go soft. If that happens, a flip tax could be deadly. Why buy into a flip tax building when there's a virtually identical non-flip tax one next door? We'd never be able to sell anything."

"I see. Do you have any other suggestions for giving the reserve fund a shot in the arm?"

"I don't think it needs it. You've been paying too much attention to Bob Carroll. He's always crying poverty, but he's just an alarmist. I think we're doing fine."

"What about the five-hundred-thousand-dollar bid that came in on the façade work?"

"I think we should refinance. I'm sure I could arrange something."

Marsh was a banker. His interest clearly lay in brokering a new mortgage for the co-op. His fee would exceed any flip tax he'd have to pay on the sale of 7A.

"Okay. Well, I'm just polling everyone to get some kind of a sense of what the sentiment is around here. Thanks for your time."

"Ida, did I show you my new acquisition?" Marsh's demeanor as ruthless banker receded into that of charming homosexual.

"No, what is it?"

"Follow me." He led her into the bedroom and with a grand sweep pointed to a ponyskin Le Corbusier chaise.

"It's gorgeous."

"Not that there's much bedroom traffic lately to admire it. The new celibacy, you know."

"It's the same old celibacy to me."

Bo Marsh walked her to the elevator and held the door in a courtly fashion. "Always a pleasure," he said.

Ida jabbed seven and pondered the situation. Maybe his anti-flip tax stance was an indication of guilt. Or maybe it was due to his obvious preference for refinancing. She just couldn't tell.

27

BOB CARROLL WOULD BE a more controlled experiment, Ida thought as she waited for him to open his door. He had brought the flip tax issue up repeatedly over the past few years. Although everyone had managed to ignore him, he had always pushed the idea. If he switched now to an anti-flip tax position, it wouldn't be too much of a stretch to assume that he intended to sell something. Quite possibly 7A.

"Come in, come in," he boomed. Although he hadn't yet looked at his watch, she already felt that she was wasting his time. "What's on the agenda?" he asked.

"Flip taxes. I'm trying to feel the board out on the idea."

"Finally someone else has come to their senses. I've been screaming flip tax for years."

"You haven't changed your mind?"

"Of course not," he said, glancing at his watch. "It's a prudent way to build up our inadequate reserve fund. It spares us the need to assess everyone. And let's face it, an assessment would never get passed. All these people wearing eight-hundred-dollar suits? We know they're all overextended. They'd probably be unable to come up with even a grand."

Ida examined Bob Carroll's suit. It was cheap, like his watch. The living room was nondescript. They sat on a faded beige sectional sofa and faced a teak wall unit that had definite undergraduate lines. Carroll was up for partner at Case & Clark next year. If he made it, maybe he'd stop complaining about being broke and buy some new furniture. Ida doubted it.

"Is there anything else you wanted to discuss?" he asked. If he couldn't bill you in six-minute intervals, he wasn't interested in talking to you. But Ida didn't want to waste the opportunity to probe a bit.

"How are things at work?"

"The same. Busy."

"When's the partnership decision coming up? Next year?"

"Uh-huh." He glanced at his watch again.

Ida sat back, hoping he would, too. He didn't. "What would you do if you made partner? What changes would you make in your life?"

"I don't know."

"Would you sell this apartment?"

"Carol and I always assumed we'd move to the suburbs and start a family." To date he'd been too cheap to have kids. His wife worked long hours as a personnel manager and he clearly didn't want to give up the income. "But Westchester's gone sky high. Even if we could get three hundred thousand for this apartment, we couldn't buy anything in a decent school district."

Ida looked at him thoughtfully. He was clearly obsessed with money. But how far would he go for it? Probably not too far, she thought. There was something buffoonish about him that precluded evil. Besides, guys like him took great pride in pleading poverty. Windfalls only upset the apple-cart. And he was still taking a pro-flip tax position. She just didn't think he was the one. Of course the Case & Clark connection was a strong indication of guilt. But it could also mean nothing. There were hundreds of lawyers there.

"Ida, I brought home a lot of work with me."

"Of course. Thanks for sparing the time to talk to me."

"So are you going to propose this at next week's board meeting? Maybe they'll listen to you."

"I want to talk to everyone first. If the other three are firmly opposed, there may be no point."

"Well, it wouldn't be a board decision, you know. We'd have to put it to a shareholder vote."

"Yes, I know," said Ida. "But if the board is lukewarm about it, the attitude will trickle down to the shareholders. Without board enthusiasm, we'll never get a flip tax passed."

"You're probably right." He strode over to the door.

"By the way, do you know anything about what's going on with the sale of seven-A? Is it on the market yet?" She watched his face closely.

"Nope," he said neutrally. His only facial expression was another glance at his watch. "See you next week." He closed the door on her.

28

"**W**HY DON'T I come up there?" Mark Sadow did not seem anxious to invite Ida into his apartment. "It's a madhouse here. The kids are screaming and we won't be able to hear ourselves talk."

"Okay." It didn't matter much to Ida. As far as getting a feeling for his apartment, she had recently had an opportunity to inspect it when she went down there to drop off a baby present. The Sadows had just had their second child. She recalled a jumble of toys and diapers, nothing that would yield a clue to guilt or innocence.

"I'll be right up," Sadow said, sounding relieved to be able to make a quick escape. He appeared at Ida's door seconds later.

"Sorry to disturb you," Ida said as she let him in, "but I'd like to discuss a flip tax proposal with you."

"Disturb me? Are you kidding? Adult conversation will be a welcome respite from what's going on down there. Anyway, why this sudden interest in flip taxes? Have you been talking to Bob Carroll again? Stay away from that man. He's trouble."

"No, actually this was my idea. I was quite alarmed at that half-million-dollar estimate we got on the façade work."

"What's in our reserve fund now?"

"Almost a million."

"So if we went ahead and had the work done, it would get knocked down to about half," he said.

"Right."

"Half a million in reserve does seem low for a pre-war building of this size. And we have potential plumbing and re-wiring costs staring us in the face."

"Maybe we should put the façade work off," Ida suggested.

"Absolutely not." Sadow sounded adamant. "It's got to be done soon. And it's got to be done right. We don't want one of those schlock jobs where they rip off the lintels and every piece of decorative trim just so they can file a clean Local Law Ten report." New York City's Local Law Ten required a façade inspection report to be filed every five years. The point was to help ferret out dangerous and hazardous conditions. The requirement had been enacted following the death of a young woman who was hit by a falling cornice.

"In an old building like this," he continued, "the top priority must always be to preserve the structure's architectural integrity." Sadow talked about architectural integrity a lot. So when Ida had read an item in last month's news about a rock star on Central Park West who had ripped out all the mahogany trim in his duplex in order to mirror the walls, she was surprised to find out that Sadow was his architect.

"So what do you think about the idea of a flip tax?"

"Maybe it's time," he said. "I had always hoped we could avoid a flip tax. I used to feel even a small maintenance increase would be preferable. But what with the second kid and all, no maintenance increase seems small to me anymore."

"I understand," said Ida sympathetically. Why don't you sell the Ferrari, you greedy bastard? she thought to herself.

"So you would support the idea of presenting a flip tax proposal to the shareholders?"

"Yes. Yes, I would. I think it's inevitable," he said. "Are you going to raise the issue at next week's board meeting?"

"I'm not sure. So far we're three for and one against. I'd like to talk to Cohen before I decide. If he's adamantly opposed, I might drop it."

"He will be," he said.

"Oh, really? How come?" Did Sadow know something she didn't know?

"He's the type who would oppose a flip tax. He hates regulation of any kind. If he weren't a Jew, he'd be a card-carrying member of the NRA." Sadow stood up. "Well, back to the loony bin."

"Try earplugs," Ida suggested as she walked him to the door. "You can buy them on most subway platforms these days."

29

"NO WAY."

Mark Sadow had been right: Mark Cohen was fiercely opposed to the idea of a flip tax.

"Why not?" asked Ida. "Do you intend to move in the foreseeable future?" She tried to keep an eye on him while she examined his living room.

"Of course I intend to move."

"To where? And when?"

"I don't know. But I certainly have no intention of spending the rest of my life in this apartment."

"You look pretty comfortable to me." Cohen lived alone. His early marriage hadn't worked out. It had been brief and there were no children. His apartment was a generously sized one-bedroom that had been professionally decorated. The decorator had used an oriental theme, perhaps to please Cohen's Japanese employers at his bank.

"Of course I'm comfortable," he said as he paced back and forth in front of his sliding shoji screens. The screens replaced the French doors that had led to the dining room. "But I hope I never get so comfortable that I stop moving forward."

"But if you have no definite plans to move, why would you be opposed to a flip tax?"

"Flip taxes are for people who are content to sit in their own shit. For little old ladies who bought at the insider price and intend to die sitting on their toilet. No offense meant, of course."

Ida smiled. "Well, I do spend a lot of time sitting on my toilet. And as I get older, toilet sitting does seem to consume more and more of my day. So I suppose there's a fairly good chance that when my last moment does come, I might very well be found there."

"Look," said Cohen, "it's a philosophical issue. It really has nothing to do with age or gender. Why should those of us with a vision be taxed in order to support those who only want to play it safe?"

"I understand what you're saying. And I admire your plans for the future. But life doesn't always work out like that, you know."

"What about subletting?" he said.

"What do you mean?"

"This month it's a flip tax that you're hot on. But last month you were all wound up about loosening up our subletting policy."

"Oh, right. I guess I'd still be interested." As soon as she found out about the murder, Ida had forgotten all about Ken's interest in purchasing and subletting Mrs. Gross's apartment.

"Now, there's something I could get behind," Cohen said enthusiastically. "I just can't stand all these restrictions forced on us just because we live in a co-op. Next time I would definitely buy a condo."

"How about a cabin in the Alaska bush?"

"I would love it."

"What keeps you in New York?" asked Ida.

"My mother," he admitted.

So the guy was a Jew after all.

"You're a good son." Ida pinched his cheek. "Just don't vote Republican," she said and ran out of there.

30

IDA'S CO-OP WAS NOT ONLY a no-subletting building, it was also a no-washing-machine building. The pipes were too old to handle the additional strain of washers and dryers in individual apartments, so everyone was supposed to use the laundry room. Of course, there were a few sneaks who had laundry facilities installed in their kitchens. But most took their dirty clothes down to the basement or over to Broadway to have them professionally done. Every year the board tackled the thorny issue of whether to invest the hundreds of thousands of dollars it would take to upgrade the plumbing. At times like this she would tend to vote yes, Ida thought, as she schlepped her laundry downstairs.

As she entered the laundry room, she was relieved to see someone else was there. Most afternoons it was creepily deserted, except for an occasional housekeeper who didn't offer much in the way of conversation. But here was Mrs. Sadow, with her baby asleep in a stroller and her toddler dancing to a tape on his Fisher Price cassette player. Mrs. Sadow looked the way mothers look after they've taken the plunge and had a second child. Mildly hysterical.

Ida loaded her machine and went over to coo at the baby. "So is it still true that two is a lot harder than one?"

"Much harder."

"It's been a long time, but I seem to remember that it does get easier."

"I'm afraid it's going to get a lot worse."

"But why? She seems like such a sweet baby. And your little boy seems happy enough."

"Right now the baby's still sleeping in our bedroom. Zachary has his own room and so does our live-in. But when Leah gets a little older, she's going to need her own room. Which means we won't have room for the live-in. Mark says we're going to have to let her go anyway. We just can't afford her."

Get him to sell the goddam Ferrari already, thought Ida, but she kept her mouth shut and just nodded.

"Besides, I really don't want to lose Lynette. She's been with me since Zachary was born, and by now I'm completely dependent on her." Mrs. Sadow leaned against one of the dryers and started to cry.

Ida tried to be comforting. "Now, I'm sure that you'll figure out an acceptable alternative."

"I never thought it would come to this. Even though I wanted a little girl, I half hoped that Leah would be a boy so that the baby could share a room with Zachary and Lynette could keep her room. And then Mark built me up with all that talk about a duplex."

A duplex? Now, which apartment did the Sadows live in? Wasn't it 6A? Of course it was. Ida remembered Sadow at last month's board meeting, worrying that the next occupant of Mrs. Gross's apartment would be jumping on his head. Just let this lady spill her guts, Ida told herself. Don't start interrogating. "A duplex?" she asked mildly.

Mrs. Sadow blew her nose. "I know he doesn't like me discussing this with anyone, but the whole thing was so unfair of him." She started to cry again. "He was so sure that we would be able to break through to the apartment above us when it became vacant. He had the plans drawn up and everything. I tried to tell him that it would be impossibly expensive. We can't even afford a housekeeper, according to him. What made him think we would ever be able to afford an entire additional apartment? Plus the renovations, even though Mark could handle the architectural work himself. But he kept saying not to worry about it, he had the whole thing figured out. And then when the old lady finally died, it seemed for a while that we would actually get our duplex. But all of a sudden Mark stopped talking about it and told me not to mention it ever again. And now we're stuffed into our apartment, and I'm losing Lynette and he still has that goddam car."

Very interesting, thought Ida. Well, she was a smart old lady, but she wasn't that smart, she told herself. If she'd been really smart, she would have written "duplex" underneath "greedy" on her oak tag.

31

WHEN NINA GOT BACK to the office from court that day, there were three messages from her mother. Nina smiled at the receptionist. "Do you think by any chance my mother wants me to call her?"

Ida picked up on the first ring. "Does the word duplex mean anything to you?" she said.

"It's a word that makes every New Yorker's heart beat a little faster. As the cowboy dreams of the range, as the Arab dreams of Mecca, we dream of a duplex."

"I meant in the context of this murder. Think about it."

"Nothing. Nothing comes to mind."

"Okay, I'll give you a hint. One of the board members lives in six-A."

"So he had Mrs. Gross killed in order to get a duplex? It sounds a little farfetched, even in this town."

Ida recounted her conversation with Mrs. Sadow in the laundry room. "I think if your friend Judah Lev interviewed Mark Sadow he'd find out some very interesting stuff. Why don't you call him with this latest bulletin?"

Ida was giving Nina a gift. Judah Lev's quiet disappearance

had upset Nina. She was breezy about it, but her mother could tell it was taking a toll, even though they had never discussed it. Nina felt as if she should say, "It's your information, you call him," but she couldn't bring herself to. Instead she jumped at the chance.

She got through on the second try and told her story quickly and breathlessly, as if she was afraid he'd hang up on her. She kept trying to sound more casual, but couldn't. This was worse than she had thought.

He liked her story, though. "Pretty impressive woman, your mother. Good sleuthing skills."

"Yeah, too bad she had to waste her life working. She would have made a great yenta."

"I'm sure she made time. What's your next move?" He was silent. She found herself blushing, but let the question hang in the air. Clarifying it would be even more embarrassing.

"We've got to get Sadow to talk," he finally said. "I'm sure he was incidental in this, that he wasn't the real master-mind. Remember, West Estates was involved in more than one murder. Besides, the fact that it's a Netherlands Antilles corporation indicates foreigners."

"How are you going to get Sadow to talk?"

"The usual way. By offering transactional immunity."

"Of course," Nina said while she furiously tried to remember what transactional immunity was. Why was it that legal terms that even laymen understood eluded her? In fact, law was one of her worst categories on "Jeopardy." And criminal law was the worst. "Of course," she repeated to break the silence. "Would you like to go away next weekend?" she said to break the next silence. My God, had she really said that? She regretted it in midsentence. How could she have been so stupid? Here was a man being deliberately elusive and she was responding just like a man-addicted jerk. Besides, she was supposed to see Grant next weekend. And Orthos didn't go away on weekends anyway, did they? Besides, where would they go? Camping? To her sister's house in the Hamptons? Both scenarios seemed improbable. She kept talking out of nervousness.

"We could rent a car, leave late on Saturday, and stay over at an inn or something. It would be nice."

This time his silence was thunderous. "I don't think so," he finally said. No excuses, no apologies, just "I don't think so." She had felt like a back-door woman from the start. But she had thought it was just God she was playing back door to. She was starting to think otherwise.

"Maybe some other time," she said politely.

"I don't think so," he said again.

Nina was in trouble. Here she was, feeling overinvolved with him while she had a five-year relationship in which she was underinvolved. Someone should write a book for her. They could call it *Women Who Love Too Much and Too Little*.

"I'll let you know as soon as I make a breakthrough with Sadow," he said.

"Fine," she said and hung up before she dug herself in any deeper.

32

NINA CALLED GRANT to make herself feel better, but he wasn't in his office. She left a message on his machine at home, where he beeped in regularly. Although he wasn't the kind of person who indulged in high-tech gadgetry, he had gotten beeper-addicted when he started doing some immigration work. He was the kind of person who gave his clients his home phone number. Nina was the kind of person who had an unlisted phone number.

He must have beeped in right away, because she got a quick call back. "I'm depressed," she told him.

"Anything that Chinese food might help cure?"

"It never hurts."

"Meet me on our bench at eight."

Some people had "our song." Grant and Nina had "our bench." The bench dated years back, from a period when Nina's intercom had been broken and Grant had grown tired of calling from the corner to be let in. So they would arrange to meet on the same Riverside Park bench instead of in Nina's apartment. One place they never met at was Grant's apartment, which was on the Lower East Side and filled with newspapers. In the beginning, they would sit on the bench and neck. Later on, the passion gave way to staring at New Jersey. But they never gave up their bench.

For a few days every year, in June, the sun lined up with the island of Manhattan so that you could see it set from any street corner just by facing west. This was one of those days, and as Nina headed over to Riverside Park that evening, she watched it drop. The park had a nineteenth-century feeling to it, and on days like this it was easy to pretend that you were in the middle of Seurat's *Sunday Afternoon on the Island of La Grande Jatte* instead of in an Upper West Side park.

Grant was waiting for her. She watched him as she approached from behind. His body was familiar to her, of course, yet it always took her by surprise. She wondered what it would feel like to have clavicles that spread out a foot from either side of your neck. Or pelvic bones that stuck out and propped up your underwear so that someone lying next to you could peek down past your elastic waist-band into your crotch. To have thighs that had never come into contact with each other and long narrow feet that could clomp up mountains effortlessly. And to smell of wood smoke even though you'd left Wisconsin fifteen years ago. It was his smell that never ceased to move her. She got a little misty as she sat down next to him.

"What's the matter?" he said, taking her hand.

"What does 'transactional immunity' mean?"

"Is that what you're crying about? That you don't know what 'transactional immunity' means?" He was happy to see her, even though she was a wreck. He was always happy to see her. For one thing, he liked getting laid. The meaningfulness of the act was not something he examined with regularity.

"I don't know why I'm crying."

"So what else is new?" He rolled his eyes.

"So what does it mean?"

"Your crying or transactional immunity?"

"Transactional immunity."

"When someone testifies before a grand jury, they get transactional immunity. Which means that they can't be prosecuted for any crime relating to the testimony they're giving. It's a way of getting people to testify."

"So the defendant doesn't usually testify before a grand jury. Otherwise he'd never get prosecuted, right?"

"Right, unless he's waived immunity. Immunity is often used for one of two codefendants, to get one to rat on the other."

Criminal law seemed to Nina to be the modern equivalent of playing electric guitar or expert joint-rolling. It was something boys were especially good at.

She took another whiff of Grant and considered never seeing him again. Was that the way this relationship was going to end? Not with a bang but a whimper? She could always marry him, she supposed. Or could she? She felt as if she were stuck in a novel with plot trouble. Chinese food might help. They headed east.

33

NINA WAS ON THE PHONE explaining transactional immunity to her mother. Actually, Ida knew quite a bit about grand juries, since several of her friends had been empaneled. Older people were often selected to sit on grand juries. They could afford the endless weeks it took out of one's life. But after all these years, grand juries still had sinister associations in Nina's mind. She had first heard of them in the sixties when people with activist ties were being subpoenaed to testify. She couldn't help but think of them as evil. When she actually had to testify in front of one, in the case of a robbery she'd witnessed, she had been surprised to find a crowd that resembled the bank line on Social Security day.

"Judah Lev thinks Sadow is the tip of the iceberg," Nina told Ida. "He's sure there are foreigners behind him, and he's trying to identify the principals of West Estates before he seeks any indictments."

"They're Japanese," Ida said.

"Are we placing bets? If so, my money's on Ferdinand Marcos."

"No, I'm serious. I'm sure they're Japanese. When you said 'foreigners,' it just clicked. I remembered that, a couple of years ago, I saw these two Japanese businessmen drive up to the building and go in. Well, you know I've been watching people come and go in that building for ages and I'd never seen any foreign business types before. Not on West End Avenue. East Forty-fifth Street, sure. But not up here. What made them even more memorable is that they got a parking space in front of the building. They pulled up, got out, and walked in, just like in the movies. You know that never happens in real life in New York. Also they were driving a BMW. I remember thinking that would make a great car ad. You know, 'Even the Japanese drive BMWs,' or something. So I followed them into the building, even though I was really on my way out, to see which bell they'd push. But the funny thing was that they had a key."

"Well, that's interesting, even if it doesn't mean anything."

"Why don't you call Judah Lev and tell him my theory?" Ida offered.

Nina stalled. "Next time I talk to him, I'll tell him about the Japanese, I promise."

"What's going on there?"

"The usual. He's sort of leaving the picture."

"These things happen. Which shouldn't mean that justice should be obstructed."

"I'll call him, I'll call him," Nina promised.

But she didn't have to. He called her an hour later. "They're Japanese," Judah Lev said as soon as she answered the phone. "Two guys. Yamaguchi and Yamamoto."

"Boy, that was quick. Sadow spilled his guts?"

"I didn't need Sadow. Before I even got to him, I had a call from the attorney general's office. West Estates registered there a couple of years ago when they bought a block of apartments in a conversion in Turtle Bay."

"And they drive a BMW." Nina told him about Ida's suspicions.

"Maybe I should hire her."

"How are you going to find these guys? Yama One and Yama Two. Are they in New York?"

"The business address on the broker-dealer statement is Myron Kaplan's office. Fortunately the form requires you to disclose your home address. And they both had Westchester addresses. Let's hope they're still there. If not, I'll have to use Sadow."

"Do you think poisoning Mrs. Gross was their idea? Or Sadow's?"

"Who knows?" he said. "I don't have enough facts yet. I've got to do more digging."

A member in good standing of the colored-pencil brigade, thought Nina. "Never mind facts. What's your gut instinct?"

"I'll reserve judgment."

"You're no fun," she said. "I'll tell you what I think. I think it was the Yamas. Sadow was just the bag man. Can't you see it? These two guys sitting around with the offering prospectus and their computers and an actuarial software program, figuring out how long they could expect Mrs. Gross and Mrs. Kahn to live. And as soon as the old ladies exceeded their life expectancy, they had to be killed. After all, one is entitled to a decent return on one's investment."

He laughed. "How about dinner?"

"When?" she asked cautiously.

"Tomorrow."

"You're very available all of a sudden."

"Yes or no?" he said.

She felt as if she had a box of chocolates in front of her. Her superego said no, but her id and her mouth said yes.

34

"I HAD SADOW IN TODAY. I'm going to have to grant him total immunity." Judah Lev brooded over his glass of Weinstock.

"How come?" Nina pulled her chair up to the restaurant table and leaned into an attentive pose.

"I sent an investigator out yesterday. The Westchester addresses were out of date. I couldn't get a lead on either Yamaguchi or Yamamoto. So I had to call in Sadow."

"What did he have to say? Did he know where the Yamas were?"

"Looks good."

"And he did hold the shares?"

"Something like that."

"So is he going to get completely off the hook?"

"Unless his wife divorces him."

"That's what happens when you cheat on your wife," Nina said.

"I didn't know he was cheating on her."

"Not cheating in the traditional sense. Not with another woman. But he wasn't playing it straight with her. He apparently never told her about his deal with the Yamas. And you can't tell your wife that you can't afford a housekeeper and expect to keep your Ferrari without being punished in some way. That's really why she spilled her guts to my mother in the laundry room, you know. She was furious with him. If it hadn't been for the rage, she would have kept her mouth shut."

"So your mother was right. It was greed that got him in trouble all the way down the line."

"You know how architects are. Only a handful make really big money. But most, no matter how well they're doing, have to spend their time surrounded by rich people, doing their bidding. It must be frustrating."

Judah Lev nodded. "Sadow told me he was sick of doing duplexes for other people. That he always wanted an internal staircase of his own. So when the Yamas approached him with this business proposition, it seemed like fate. Look, I shouldn't be telling you this. So keep a lid on it, okay?"

"Ooh, an Ortho who talks like a character in a Raymond Chandler novel. Very appealing. Well, the moral of the story is that you can screw your clients, you can screw your partners, but don't try to screw your wife."

"I'll keep that in mind."

"Why? Do you have a wife?"

Judah Lev paused. "Nina, there's something I've been wanting to talk to you about."

She recognized his tone of voice. She'd seen enough men come and go to be able to spot one who was on his way out.

She put on her good-sport demeanor. "What's up?"

"I'll probably be getting married soon."

She felt as if she'd been kicked in the stomach. But not kicked hard enough to kill her curiosity. "Who is she?"

"Her name is Mindy Wolf."

"What does she do?"

"What do you mean?"

"What do you mean what do I mean? What does Mindy Wolf do for a living?"

"Nothing."

"What do you mean nothing?" Her good-sport voice was being replaced by a bad-sport shriek.

"She just graduated from college."

"You mean to tell me that you're marrying a teenager, for chrissakes?"

"Calm down. She's not a teenager. She's twenty-one years old."

"Where did you meet this child?"

"She's a member of the congregation at Lincoln Square. I've known her parents for years."

"Where does she live?"

"Central Park West. In the sixties."

"Oh, my God. Of course. Money. Why do I always forget about money? I'm the only person in the world who forgets to think about it. I should have a little tattoo on the palm of my hand that says 'Don't forget to think about money.' "

"Look, Nina, Mindy is a lovely, sweet person. It's true that she's very sheltered, but I'm sure she'll be a good wife and mother."

"What can I say? I guess you know what you're doing. Everybody seems to, except me."

"I thought it best to tell you now. I didn't want you to get upset this Sunday. I know how carefully you read the wedding and engagement announcements."

"You mean you're getting married this weekend?"

"No, but the engagement announcement is going to be in."

"How loaded is she, anyway? You might as well let me know now and prepare me for the pain of reading in the *Times* about her family's vast holdings."

"They're in real estate."

"Don't tell me you're marrying a Wolf. As in Wolf Associates?"

"Her father is Morris Wolf."

Nina was hurt and shocked. But also impressed. "Holy shit, Judah Lev. Mazel tov. If you're going to sell your soul, sell it for big bucks." She signaled the waiter. It was clearly time to get the check.

35

JUDAH LEV AND NINA were going to be friends. It always made Nina sick, that being friends business. Once it was over, she never wanted to see any of them again. She considered it a triumph if she could be in the same room with one of them. Friends was asking too much. But sometimes being friends was useful, and she was damned if she and Ida were going to be gypped out of watching the Yamas get caught. After a plea was entered or a verdict reached, then she could tell him that she never wanted to see him again.

Actually it turned out to be easy to get information out of Judah Lev. Since he had clarified their relationship, he seemed much more comfortable. He called her every day, chatting amiably, keeping her posted. When she met him for a drink he was warm and affectionate. Now that they weren't seeing each other anymore, they made a great couple.

And his daily bulletins were promising. Sadow was great in front of the grand jury. There was no trouble getting an indictment. Judah Lev had been in contact with the Yamas and they seemed anxious to enter a plea. Case & Clark was representing them. It would be a fun case to try, but it probably wouldn't go to trial. The exterminator had independent counsel but also seemed anxious to plea-bargain. Judah Lev promised Nina a detailed debriefing session as soon as pleas were entered.

When the moment finally came, Judah Lev chose his office to debrief in. Nina suspected that she could have gotten more out of him over a bottle of Weinstock, but she didn't object. He didn't actually have to tell her anything if he didn't want to. But he proved forthcoming.

"Tell me everything," she said. "From the beginning."

"In the beginning, there were the Yamas. Two executives for a Japanese importing firm. The Tokyo office had assigned them to New York for a couple of years. Their wives stayed behind in Japan, so they shared an apartment that the firm had rented in a building on East Forty-eighth Street. When the building converted, the firm was offered the right to buy at the insider's price, but only if they designated an individual to hold the shares. The firm was a corporation, and since the apartment was being sold to the occupant, the shares would not be unsold shares. Before the tax law changed, everything except unsold shares had to be held by an individual from the start. For basically the same reason it was necessary to designate an individual to hold unsold shares three years after closing. The Internal Revenue code required it."

"This is incredibly boring so far," Nina said. "It sounds like a tax lecture, not a murder."

"You can leave if you'd like."

"I suppose this is what life and death is like these days. The Business section instead of the tabloids."

"Shall I go on?"

"Please do."

"Anyway, the Yamas were designated to hold the shares allocated to their apartment, and they became interested in the conversion. The sponsor offered them several occupied apartments at reduced rates. Like good businessmen, they looked not only into the resale value of the apartments but also into the profile of the tenants occupying the units. Since it was a non-eviction plan, they would have to wait for the tenants to die or move before they could sell the apartment unoccupied. They naturally chose the apartments with the oldest tenants. That way they'd be able to realize a return on their investment more quickly."

"Did they buy the apartments as individuals or as West Estates?"

"As West Estates. They felt that their employer would probably disapprove of their investing on their own. You know how those Japanese corporations are. They own you body and soul for life. So the Yamas created West Estates and incorporated in the Netherlands Antilles so that the firm would never find out."

"So the name West Estates had nothing to do with West End Avenue?"

"No, they called themselves West Estates because they saw themselves as easterners owning a little chunk of the West as their estate. Anyway, they bought a bunch of apartments in the building, getting a great discount, but then they found out that a buyer of a block of apartments had to register with the attorney general's office as a purchaser for investment or resale. If they bought only one apartment in a building, they didn't have to register. So from then on, they bought single units to preserve their anonymity."

"And that's how you got those Westchester addresses? From their registration with the attorney general when they bought on Forty-eighth Street?"

"Right."

"But what were they doing with Westchester addresses if they were living on the East Side?"

"The importing firm sold the apartment the Yamas had been living in. Although the firm had designated them to hold the shares, the corporation actually owned it. To induce the Yamas to agree to sell the apartment, the firm let them bring their wives over and moved them to Westchester. Meanwhile, within a year of investing in the block of apartments, an elderly tenant died and the Yamas flipped the apartment and tripled their money. They were ecstatic. They started hunting around for apartments occupied by non-purchasing little old ladies. It seemed like a sure thing. Except that none of the subsequent tenants were as cooperative as the first one. They just hung on and on. And West Estates found themselves shelling out for mortgage and maintenance costs and losing a fortune. It got to the point where the tax write-off wasn't doing them any good because they had no income to offset. Before they knew it, three years were almost up and it would be necessary to designate an individual to hold the shares."

"So they decided to take matters into their own hands?" Nina was happy. Now they were getting to the good part.

"Right. They knew that sudden deaths would be less suspicious when the corpse was eighty-five years old. And fortunately, they had always been very careful to preserve the anonymity of West Estates since they were still working for the import firm. That's why they took such precautions with their lawyers."

"Yeah, what was that all about? I never understood that business with Myron Kaplan and Case and Clark."

"Myron Kaplan was some sleaze bag they had met while negotiating a deal for the importing firm. He seemed like the kind of guy who put a major emphasis on client confidentiality, if you know what I mean. So they took him into their confidence, and he represented them in all of West Estates' business. Except he wouldn't go to court. He was phobic. Case and Clark represented the importing firm on corporate matters, so the Yamas were known there. They persuaded their attorney at Case and Clark to send a young litigator to court for them. It's something the big firms will do for corporate clients as a favor. You know, they'll get you a divorce, close on your house, bail you out on a criminal charge, that kind of stuff. As long as you keep giving them your corporate business. Case and Clark is also representing the Yamas on the criminal charges."

"Whatever happened to Myron Kaplan?"

"He's completely disappeared. The Yamas claim they have no idea what happened to him."

"And you believe them?"

"I do."

"Enough about lawyers. What about the murder?"

"Well, they hired some guy who was sort of a failed hit man to stick digitalis into the old ladies' food. He was glad to have the work. Apparently he was one of those people who had never minded the thought of killing people, but he just couldn't stand violence. This was perfect for him. The Yamas had him genuinely exterminate the apartment while he was at it, figuring that as long as the stuff actually got rid of the roaches, the tenants wouldn't complain. He'd be able to come and go as often as he needed to."

Nina nodded. "That's true. In New York no one's going to throw out an exterminator who actually gets rid of roaches. It's like throwing Raquel Welch out of bed or something."

"Or something. So the exterminator would put the digitalis powder in kitchen items that had already been opened. He wasn't careful enough to make sure that none of the digitalis spilled over into the exterminating powder."

"Which is why there were digitalis traces in the cabinets."

"Right. Both powders were white, so it was harder to tell. And since the digitalis was white, he usually stuck to light powdery foods. Flour, sugar, stuff like that. And it worked. Kahn and Gross weren't the first, you know."

"How many in all?"

"Five. This is what they'd do. They'd buy apartments with old ladies living in them. If the tenant didn't die of natural causes within the first two years, they'd use the exterminator. That way they'd get rid of the old lady before the three years were up and they had to designate an individual to hold the shares. Once they designated themselves as individuals their anonymity would be blown."

"It doesn't seem like there would be enough money in this to make it worth their while."

"Think about it. Five victims. They made at the very least two hundred thousand per apartment. That's a million dollars minimum. The first was an old German lady in Yorkville. Then they got someone on Central Park West."

"That reminds me. I assume Mrs. Singer has been warned. As in West Estates versus Singer."

"Of course. Luckily she's been in Florida and out of danger. Anyway, everything went according to plan until they came up against Mrs. Gross. They had high hopes for that apartment. Its value had increased tremendously, and the exterminator assured them that he had no trouble sneaking the digitalis into Mrs. Gross's sugar bowl. But she just wouldn't die. They never figured her for a health nut. That sugar bowl was there for company, which fortunately never came. She herself never went near it. Almost three years had passed and they knew they'd have to sell the apartment to avoid designating an individual. But they couldn't bring themselves to sell it. They were sure that Mrs. Gross was going to kick any minute. And they were greedy after having made a couple hundred thousand on some other little old lady on West End Avenue. The one after Central Park West but before Kahn and Gross.

"This is when Sadow came into the picture?"

"Yup. They very discreetly contacted Mark Sadow."

"How did they know they could trust him to maintain their precious anonymity?"

"Well, at first they revealed very little. Not even their names. They just told him that they owned the apartment above his as a corporation and needed someone to hold the shares for them. In return, when the apartment became vacant, they would sell it to him at a greatly reduced price."

"Why did they choose him?"

"It seemed reasonable that someone with a contiguous apartment might be interested in expanding. And Mrs. Gross had an old lady on top of her and another old lady on one side of her. Your mother, that is. And old ladies don't think about duplexes. On the other side of Gross was the elevator shaft and compactor room. So that left Sadow."

"Wasn't he suspicious about their needing a total stranger to hold the shares?"

"Of course. He's not stupid. And he used his suspicions as a bargaining chip in his price negotiations. They ultimately agreed to deliver the apartment vacant at three hundred thousand. An extremely low price for what it was."

"So Sadow knew there was something unusual about the transaction?"

"He certainly did. He was doing a deal with the devil, and he knew it. But for half-price there were no questions asked. Meanwhile, the Yamas were still making about a hundred grand, since selling the apartment with Mrs. Gross living in it would only have gotten them about two hundred thousand."

"So everything went smoothly after that?"

"Pretty much. Sadow was getting impatient, though. He had been hoping to have his duplex by the time his second child was born. So the exterminating efforts were stepped up. The guy gave up on the sugar bowl and started putting the digitalis into everything that was open. And made more frequent visits. Which explains why a freshly opened box of matzoh meal was so quickly tainted. When Mrs. Gross finally died, all parties were greatly relieved. But cautious. They didn't want anyone to know that Sadow already had the shares. It would look too suspicious. So they made a big show of putting the apartment on the market. That's why the broker showed it to you."

"And Mrs. Kahn's apartment?"

"That really was on the market. The Yamas planned on selling it. But on Gross's, they were going to do a bogus transfer to Sadow, who already held the shares."

"But wouldn't someone inspecting the board's records realize that Sadow had owned it all along?"

"No, because a fictitious individual had been designated as shareholder. They called him Westmark, a combination of West Estates and Mark Sadow. Sadow was able to record the phony entry in the ledger book and issue mock shares to Mr. Westmark. Meanwhile, the real shares, which were in Sadow's name, were held in escrow by the Yamas. The agreement was that once Gross died and Sadow paid the three hundred thousand, the shares would be released to him. Then they would pretend to have a closing where title passed from Westmark to Sadow. No one would ever know that Sadow had held the shares all along."

"Very clever."

"Except that you and your mother discovered a murder. Then Sadow freaked out. He had known all along that something wasn't kosher, but this was more than he had bargained for. So he inked out the Westmark entry in the ledger book and stole the apartment file. And hoped the whole thing would go away, that the Yamas would walk away from the apartment and remain untraceable, and that no one would connect him with the whole deal. Remember, he had nothing invested. All he had done was agree to hold the shares. So he wouldn't really be losing anything."

"Except his dream of a duplex."

"Right. He was sorely disappointed. His one big shot at wealth was gone."

"So he took it out on his wife."

"What do you mean?"

"It's clear," said Nina. "He was feeling bitter and broke. So he put the screws on Mrs. Sadow, trying to cut back on the child care. And the thought of being alone with two small children all day put her over the edge. Made her tell the whole story to some sympathetic old lady in the laundry room. What were the Yamas doing all this time?"

"They were at a loss. Kaplan had disappeared, so they just kept paying the maintenance through their computer until they could figure out what to do." Judah Lev looked at his watch. "It's late, I've really got to go. This getting-married business is very time-consuming."

"I'm sure it is." Nina stood.

He walked her to the door and put his hand on her arm, looking into her eyes. "Nina, I'm glad we'll be able to remain friends."

She looked back into his eyes. "Judah Lev, I never want to see you again."

36

NINA FLIPPED OFF HER SHOES as she flopped into one of the chaises on the deck. The Hamptons were boring but restorative. She never wanted to see another man. She could barely even look at her brother-in-law, who was politely sitting and listening as she recounted the end of the Yama saga.

"So what happens to the apartment now?" he asked.

"I don't know," said Nina.

"Does it get auctioned off like a car caught in a drug bust?" he asked.

"He means can he get a deal," said Laura from the garden.

"Yeah, can I get a deal?"

Nina shrugged. "I don't know what'll happen. You can't really impound an apartment, can you?" She stared into her iced tea and watched the fresh mint float on top. "Laura, where did you get the mint from? The garden?"

"Uh-huh." Laura came back up onto the deck. "We're growing spearmint and peppermint this year. And I just put in some apple mint out of curiosity." Laura was wearing a suspiciously oversized cotton jumper that didn't look as loose as it should around the waist.

"You're pregnant again, aren't you?" Nina said.

Laura smiled. "I'm due in January. But I didn't want to announce it yet. Don't tell Ma, okay?"

"Okay." Nina looked at her sister. Great legs, three kinds of fresh mint, and now three kids, too. And a rather pedestrian worldview that seemed less of a detriment and more of a benefit as the years went on.

"I've made a decision," Nina said. "I'm either going to marry Grant or not marry him."

"What kind of a decision is that?" said Laura.

"A Nina kind of decision," said Ken.

"Really, it's going to be one or the other," Nina said. "I'm getting too old for all this. When Judah Lev told me he was going to marry that real-estate heiress, I told myself that this was the last time I would be party to such a scene. I just don't have the ability to snap back the way I used to."

"We're all losing our elasticity," said Laura, jiggling her belly gently.

"So I've decided. I'm either going to marry Grant or find someone else to marry. Fast."

"Well, it's good you've made a decision," said Laura. "But don't you still have to decide which you're going to do?"

"That's the only problem." Nina chewed on her mint sprig. "I just can't decide."

37

SHE HAD DECIDED. It was hard telling Grant, but it would have been just as hard telling him to marry her. He had taken it the way he took an order of eviction for one of his clients. He argued a bit, but basically knew it wasn't worth appealing.

She sent him home with a stack of his underwear and shirts. For the first week she kept noticing the gap they left in her closet. She felt like one of those recently divorced women who stare at the white strip on their finger where their wedding band used to be. Then she got over it. She did all those things that single women of a certain type did. She went hiking with the Appalachian Mountain Club, signed up for theater subscriptions, saw films at the Museum of Modern Art. She even went on a folk dance weekend with Ida in the Catskills. Even though she gained three pounds she still had fun. Nina made a remarkably good old maid.

The only thing she didn't like was having to try to find men. Grant had served a function. He obviated the need to date. Now that she had proclaimed that she was looking for a husband, there was nobody around. She waited for that little stomach flip that let her know she was attracted to someone, but it never came. She kept thinking about this old episode of "Taxi" where Marilu Henner tells Judd Hirsch about this really cute guy who got into the back of her cab that day. He seemed nice, but she's no dummy. In this town, she knows he's got to be married, gay, or crazy. "C'mon, crazy!" she says, as if she's at a horse race.

Sometimes Nina thought about Judah Lev. One Saturday morning as she was schlepping her groceries home from the Red Apple, she saw him in front of the Lincoln Square Synagogue. He was with a pregnant woman who was clearly Mindy Wolf Lev. Funny, Nina didn't know Nipon made maternity clothes. She crossed the street to avoid them.

One thing that improved was her work. Now that Grant wasn't around to tell her how much she should like housing court, the place seemed more tolerable to her. She even indulged in a bit of impact litigation. In the past she had avoided federal and class action suits. She didn't like to write briefs she couldn't fit on the back of an envelope. But this time she found herself very involved with a client who had been illegally evicted. The marshal had thrown all of the woman's things down the stairs and what wasn't broken had later been lost in storage. Nina helped the woman bring a federal civil rights action against the marshal and the landlord. It was an unusually ambitious project for her, but seemed the only way to even begin to compensate the woman for her damages.

She was nervous about appearing in federal court. She expected to find the place insufferably stuffy. But it turned out to be a real classy joint. She loved the glowing wood, the high ceilings. She even loved the white guys in their navy blue suits. They spoke in calm, well-modulated voices and communicated articulately, instead of the screaming that went on in housing court. It was like graduating from her South Bronx junior high school and getting to Bronx Science. There she had kept expecting her teachers to start screaming, but they never did. Federal court was the same way. Quiet and sane.

The judge assigned to her case had a kind and intelligent face. She liked the way he kibitzed in a dignified manner. He looked about forty-five, with a generous nose and a halo of frizzy hair that had receded just a bit. He reminded her of those guys who had lived on the West Side for twenty-five years and bought herring at Murray's and had a regular poker game and sent their kids to P.S. 87. He wasn't wearing a wedding band.

Her opposing counsel was a man named Graves from a big Wall Street firm. She got into an argument with him about a briefing schedule. He wanted an impossibly early return date. She appealed to the judge. "Your Honor, I need more time."

"We've already been overly generous with time," Graves said. "Ms. Fischman should be aware that this court has an obligation to expedite these matters as swiftly as possible."

"That's my concern, not yours," said the judge. "Ms. Fischman, how much time do you need?"

"You must keep in mind, Your Honor, that I work for a legal services office with limited resources. We do not have a round-the-clock staff of secretaries and paralegals, as my opposing counsel does. I'll need at least eight weeks if I'm to adequately represent my client."

"Eight weeks?" He gave her a smile that went straight to her gut. She couldn't believe it. She was actually being flirted with by a federal judge. And she felt her stomach flip as he said, "Ms. Fischman, please approach the bench."